Her Sister's Tattoo

"*Her Sister's Tattoo* is all about a family with a multigenerational passion for political activism, but the narrator's voice is always clear and calm. Meeropol writes with precision, insight and compassion about the most tumultuous moments in human life, whether they happen in public or in private. Above all, she artfully invents a fictional story that enables readers to penetrate some of the agonies and mysteries of a very real case."
—Jonathan Kirsch, *Jewish Journal*

"One of the great pleasures in reading *Her Sister's Tattoo* lies in its attention to the five senses, from patchouli in the air at the opening protest to a child drawing on newsprint with "four fat crayons" to the sight of origami cranes. An exploration about how we make decisions on where our loyalties lie."—Bethanne Patrick, *LitHub*

"The themes explored in the book—loyalty, conflicting decisions, right vs wrong, social justice, family relationships— . . . are some of the most challenging interpersonal issues we humans grapple with. The success of *Her Sister's Tattoo* is that Meeropol has managed to approach difficult issues with a keen sensitivity. Finding this particular book at this particular time in history seemed quite serendipitous, as all of us confront difficulties during our own national time of crisis."—Tracey Barnes Priestley, *Times Standard*

Kinship of Clover

"*Kinship of Clover* advances a deep appreciation of difference and of the bonds of love that provide sustenance in a fracturing, threatened world. It is a wondrous example of how a political novel, in the right hands, can achieve high artistry."—Céline Keating, *Necessary Fiction*

"If a novel can serve as both a harbinger of the future and a parable for our fraught political times, then Ellen Meeropol has done it again."
—Lisa C. Taylor, *Midwest Book Review*

"Ellen Meeropol's new novel, *Kinship of Clover*, is heartbreaking and haunting, with a cast of finely drawn and deeply memorable characters."—Frank O. Smith, *Portland Press Herald*

On Hurricane Island

"*On Hurricane Island* is a chilling, Kafkaesque story about what happens when the United States does to citizens at home what it has done to others abroad. Meeropol puts the reader right into the middle of these practices through characters about whom you really care, and a story you can't put down."—Michael Ratner, Center for Constitutional Rights

"I didn't expect to find myself reading a page-turner, but that's really what the novel is—and aspires to be. The novel forces us to contemplate things we'd rather not think could be true, and wonder. . . . The novel's stark but clear setting rose to character status, and its very cinematic descriptions of action were clear enough to watch events unfold. That's to say I found myself casting the movie in my head; I think you will, too."
—Sarah Werthan Buttenwieser, *Valley Advocate*

House Arrest

"Meeropol raises bold questions and allows her handful of main characters to debate the merits: What constitutes a family, and who decides which variations qualify? When is it acceptable to bend the rules, and at what expense? Is it possible to separate actions from consequences? . . . This multi-genre novel defies easy classification. Part medical mystery, morality tale and psychological drama, it's above all a terrific read."
—Joan Silverman, *The Portland Press Herald*

"[A]n original, riveting, and suspenseful yet warm and sensitive story that deftly explores the concepts of right and wrong, the unequal balance between rigid law and common sense, the unintended consequences of political activism, and the decisions people make when faced with tough life choices."—William D. Bushnell, *The New Maine Times*

"In this strong first novel, an unusual relationship develops between a home-care nurse and the pregnant cult member under house arrest to whom she is assigned prenatal visits . . . Meeropol's work is thoughtful and tightly composed, unflinching in taking on challenging subjects and deliberating uneasy ethical conundrums."—*Publishers Weekly*
(starred review)

THE LOST WOMEN OF
AZALEA COURT

a novel

Ellen Meeropol

🐓 Red Hen Press | *Pasadena, CA*

Book design by Mark E. Cull

Library of Congress Cataloging-in-Publication Data

Names: Meeropol, Ellen, author.
Title: The lost women of Azalea Court : a novel / Ellen Meeropol.
Description: First Edition. | Pasadena, CA: Red Hen Press, 2022.
Identifiers: LCCN 2022006687 (print) | LCCN 2022006688 (ebook) | ISBN
    9781636280493 (paperback) | ISBN 9781636280509 (ebook)
Classification: LCC PS3613.E375 L67 2022 (print) | LCC PS3613.E375
    (ebook) | DDC 813/.6—dc23
LC record available at https://lccn.loc.gov/2022006687
LC ebook record available at https://lccn.loc.gov/2022006688

The National Endowment for the Arts, the Los Angeles County Arts Commission,
the Ahmanson Foundation, the Dwight Stuart Youth Fund, the Max Factor Family
Foundation, the Pasadena Tournament of Roses Foundation, the Pasadena Arts &
Culture Commission and the City of Pasadena Cultural Affairs Division, the City of
Los Angeles Department of Cultural Affairs, the Audrey & Sydney Irmas Charitable
Foundation, the Kinder Morgan Foundation, the Meta & George Rosenberg
Foundation, the Allergan Foundation, the Riordan Foundation, Amazon Literary
Partnership, and the Mara W. Breech Foundation partially support Red Hen Press.

First Edition
Published by Red Hen Press
www.redhen.org

This novel is dedicated to Rebecca and Zelda and William and Harriet, and all the other ill, lost, and inconvenient residents of Northampton State Hospital.

THE LOST WOMEN OF
AZALEA COURT

Author's Note

The Lost Women of Azalea Court is a work of fiction. The Northampton State Hospital treated patients from 1858 to 1993, but Azalea Court and its inhabitants exist only on these pages. Names, characters, places, and events are either the product of my imagination or are used fictitiously. Any resemblance to actual persons, living or dead, or to businesses or institutions, is coincidental and unintended.

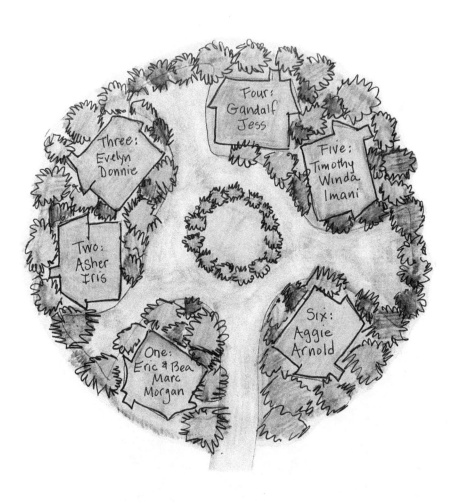

THE WOMEN

Everything changed when Iris went missing.

Before that morning, if you had asked anyone living in the six bungalows on Azalea Court if we were close, we would have rolled our eyes. We're not one of those neighborhoods that celebrate holidays with grab bag gift exchanges or host cheerful red, white, and blue progressive dinners where you have appetizers at one house and off to another for the next course. We mostly respect each other's privacy and stay in our own homes and yards.

That is, until Iris disappeared.

People often ask us if Azalea Court is cursed. "How could it not be?" they insist. It's a balloon-on-a-string shaped road, though that description implies celebration and fun and that's not really us. Our small homes sit on the grounds of the former state mental hospital, where thousands of lost souls were incarcerated over the course of a century and a half. By the time our six wood-frame bungalows were built on the edge of the hospital grounds to house medical staff and their families, the state hospital was no longer burdened with "insane" or "lunatic" in its title, but it was still regarded with deep suspicion by the town. A developer renovated the houses in the early 1950s, and another repurposed them as condos fifty years later when the nearby Hospital Hill neighborhood was constructed.

Long after the last patients were transferred out and the crumbling red brick buildings torn down or gutted for apartments, the stigma persisted. "How can you live there?" asked our classmates in high school and acquaintances in the grocery store. They rarely waited for an answer.

Tucked away in a swamp maple grove, our small court with its center circle of grass triggered suspicion in town; they read our secluded
location as unsociable. Azalea Court is not easy to find, if you don't already know it. Because the court is hidden from the road and accessed
by a narrow lane off Prince Street, looking for the street sign is unreli-
able. For some unfathomable reason, stealing it is a time-honored tra-
dition of the high school football team. We sometimes joke about how
many local teens have a green metal Azalea Court sign swinging from
a nail on their bedroom wall. Some of us feel that the petty vandalism
is aimed at the state hospital and specifically at those of us who once
worked there, but others say we're just being paranoid.

In spite of the complicated history, we like living on Azalea Court.
Thanks to Eric's horticultural prowess, our postage-stamp front yards
are exuberant with blooms, in stark contrast to the crumbling decay of
the institutional buildings finally torn down. Butterfly bushes, spiky
bee balm, a pastel rainbow of azaleas, and thick laurel shrubs threaten
our wood porch structures. Magnolias litter their wanton petals onto
our parked cars. Most of us let down our hair in our private backyards,
where patios open up to wooden play structures, croquet sets, teak
picnic tables with striped market umbrellas and pot-bellied clay stoves
that inevitably crack after a year or two.

We neighbors are a mixed group, so it's not surprising that we don't
socialize much. Our gardener/caretaker lives in Number One with his
fancy doctor wife and their two school-aged kids. Our local celebrity,
Dr. Asher Blum, who is really more infamous than famous, lives at
Number Two with his wife Iris, the person at the center of the current
trouble. Dr. Blum was the last head shrink at the state hospital, the guy
who oversaw the dismantling of the institution after working there for
decades. Rumor has it that he's writing a book about the state hospital
and the history of the institutional treatment of the mentally ill. He
calls it "What We Thought We Knew," and many of us are more than a
little worried about what nasty surprises he might reveal, what unpleasant publicity it might bring to disrupt our privacy on Azalea Court.

At ninety-four, Blum is the oldest resident, but he's not the person who has lived here the longest. That would be our neighbor Donnie, who was born in Number Three and still lives there now with his wife Evelyn, the neighborhood gossip. Donnie inherited his house from his mother, who bought the place with decades of deductions from her wages as an attendant on the women's locked ward. We've heard that the people who once lived in Number Four had a hot tub in back and used it naked, but none of us ever saw them and they moved away five years ago. Now people gossip about the lesbian couple living there. Not because of their sexual orientation—nothing unusual about that in this city—but they keep strictly to themselves, and we've heard whispers about the Witness Protection Program. Number Five stands empty, although a couple with a baby is supposedly moving in any day now. None of us is friendly with the folks in Number Six, even though they've rented their cottage for years from the college just across the river. It's too bad, but they just don't fit in. An oversized American flag flies in their front yard, the guy has odd eyes and never talks to anyone, and the androgynous-looking woman is rarely seen, and never without a hoodie.

If you could see directly into our hearts and read our secrets, you'd know that in addition to the ugly, ancient secrets of the hospital, our little street is home to people who have survived all sorts of trauma, from genocide to rape to kidnapping to torture. But on that Friday morning in November 2019 when Iris went missing, Azalea Court was quietly sliding out of autumn and anticipating winter. It was the last place any of us expected to see police cars and search teams.

FRIDAY MORNING

What We Thought We Knew:

I proceed, gentlemen, briefly to call your attention to the present state of insane persons confined within this Commonwealth, in cages, closets, cellars, stalls, pens! Chained, naked, beaten with rods, and lashed into obedience.

—Dorothea Dix,
speaking to the Legislature of Massachusetts, 1843

LEXI BLUM

Lexi's mother went missing on a cloudy Friday morning in November. Her parents' next-door neighbor telephoned around eleven.

"You'd better come right away," Eric said. "The cops are here. Your mother is gone, must have wandered off."

Her mother had become increasingly vague and forgetful over the past month. Her father didn't believe in consulting any other health professional. He diagnosed his wife's condition as Alzheimer's and insisted he was perfectly capable of managing her care.

Lexi told her co-workers she had a family emergency and sped the three-plus miles to Azalea Court. A city police cruiser blocked the narrow lane, so she drove past the blocked entrance, continued on Prince Street, and turned into the Community Gardens to park on the gravel road. Turning off the engine, she wondered about her mother wandering off. It wasn't uncommon in people with dementia, but Lexi wasn't convinced Iris *had* dementia. Her mom had been acting strange the past few weeks. Forgetful and vague, yes, but also unhappy and evasive and secretive.

She unfastened her seat belt but didn't move, staring at the back of her parents' house beyond the garden and the cruisers. She tried to slow-breathe through the worry, but she couldn't make herself get out of the car.

Lexi's parents had moved to Azalea Court in August 1953, two months after the Rosenbergs were executed—her mother told her that many times, always in a whisper as if the FBI was listening in. Iris had certain things she was religiously passionate about, even though she hadn't been inside a synagogue for decades. One of those things was putting a menorah in the bay window of Number Two and silently lighting the right number of candles. Another was more recent and involved refusing to help her husband with the book he was writing. "It's your version of heaven and hell," she told him. "I don't want any part of it."

Living on Azalea Court was okay when Lexi was young. Donnie next door was the same age and the two of them ran happily wild on the state hospital grounds. They climbed the old copper beech trees and strung ropes and pulleys across the Mill River to exchange secret messages back and forth in tin buckets. Their favorite activity was sneaking into the hospital buildings after dark. They called it 'adventuring.' They vaguely understood that the hospital was a sad place, and that the people confined there were sick in different ways, but never thought about it much beyond that. One time they stole fresh baked brownies from the kitchen. Some spring evenings they watched as girls in pastel skirts came in a bus from the women's colleges to dance and flirt with the patients and staff. "Community service," her mother explained when Lexi asked about it. Then one night, the summer they were ten, while searching for an entrance to the mythical underground tunnels that connected the hospital buildings, Donnie and Lexi stumbled on a male attendant moving around on top of a patient whose nightgown was pulled up to cover her face. They never talked about it, but that was the last time they went adventuring at the hospital. Lexi moved out of her parents' home at Two Azalea Court when she was eighteen and never lived there again.

Lexi was not proud of how long she sat in her car that morning, unable to face her father. But she finally pulled herself together, as he had taught her when she flipped out about solving algebra equations in seventh grade or left a science project until the weekend before it was due. "Pull yourself together and do the right thing," he'd say.

Walking through the Community Gardens, Lexi marveled at how some people carefully prepared their plots for winters and others just left the detritus of the harvest to fend for itself under the coming snow and ice. There might be a useful metaphor there, but if so, she couldn't find it. Landscapes and gardens were her business, but she blocked out her professional gaze as she walked, surveying the patchwork squares in browns and beige, just in case her mother rested on a frozen bench under someone's shriveled grape arbor or huddled between barrels stuffed with shovels and rakes and watering cans waiting for spring.

Lexi always knew something was different about her family. When she was little, she understood that her father had a sadness inside. He was older than her friends' fathers, less likely to get down on the floor and build windmills with Tinker Toys. She wondered why her parents didn't have a big family of aunts and uncles and cousins like Donnie's family or raucous parties with college friends like the people who used to live in Number Four. She also wondered why she didn't have a brother or sister. Oh, how she wanted a sister! That would make the family more balanced, more even: two parents and two kids.

Maybe it was her lack of extended family or close friends that made her so curious about Harriet. Lexi was fifteen when she discovered Harriet. She shouldn't have been snooping in her mother's things, but Iris was at a PTA meeting and her father was watching a news show and wouldn't let Lexi change the channel to anything interesting. Bored and lonely, she sat at her mother's dressing table and tried on her necklaces and silly clip-on earrings. The photo was in the bottom of Iris's pink satin jewelry box, under her favorite string of pearls. Her mother looked so young and happy it made Lexi's throat ache. Elbows linked, her young mom and a curly-haired stranger stood grinning widely in front of an old-timey shack with a sign that said FERRY. On the back, written in her mother's careful script: *Harriet and me, 1949*. Lexi carried the photo into the living room and waved it at her father.

"Who's Harriet?"

He looked up. His eyes darted from Lexi's face to the photograph in her hand and back to the TV. "Where'd you get that?"

"In Mom's jewelry box," she said. "Who's Harriet?"

"Give me that. It's not yours."

She rolled her eyes. It was her response of choice that year. "Not yours either. Who is Harriet?"

"You shouldn't have taken that," her father said. "Your mother will be furious."

"Who *is* she?"

"Who?"

"Harriet!" She hated it when he got like that. Purposely vague. "Stop acting stupid," Lexi said. "She was Mom's friend?"

He hesitated, then said, "Her best friend, from growing up on the island."

"So how come I've never met her, never even heard of her?"

"We don't talk about it. Those were terrible years."

"Why? What happened?"

Her father turned up the volume and held out his hand. "We lost track of her years ago. Give me the photograph. And never bring her name up again. For your mother's sake."

Lexi stared at his face, trying to read his expression. Reluctantly, she handed him the photo.

She had no idea why she thought about Harriet now, decades later, as she walked slowly towards her parents' home. She wished she had kept that photo and asked her mother about it. She only knew that her parents had some sort of important secret and it involved Harriet. But it was nothing that could help now that her mother was missing.

A uniformed policeman stood at attention on the porch. Her father was a private man and would hate having a cop at his door. Maybe he was hiding something, perhaps he felt guilty about something bad from long ago, but he was still her dad and she loved him anyway. How could she hold *both* of those things in her heart? She felt sorry for him too, on top of worrying like crazy about her mother.

What a mess. But Eric's phone call didn't surprise her. Lexi had always half-expected something awful to be revealed about her parents, about her father. Standing on the sidewalk and watching the uniformed cop on their front porch, she couldn't bring herself to climb the steps. Lexi loved her parents, of course she did. But her mother hadn't been herself recently, and her father had never been an easy guy.

Somebody had to be his daughter, but this was not the first time she wished that somebody wasn't her.

ERIC GOLDEN

Eric peered out his front window at Lexi Blum, standing motionless on the sidewalk in front of her parents' home. Red and blue lights from the police cruiser flashed a syncopated strobe pattern onto her beige jacket. Why was she just standing there instead of going inside? Wasn't she anxious to hear the details about her mother?

He pressed his wife's photo on the children's gadget phone. Bea had pasted photos on the fat buttons—her own on top, then Eric's—so their kids could reach them easily in an emergency. Why couldn't the kids memorize the numbers or look at a list, like kids did when he was little? Besides, he was always home.

Bea's voicemail didn't pick up right away. Maybe for once she remembered to turn her cell phone back on when she finished her morning surgery schedule.

"What's up?" Bea's voice was muffled. He pictured her chewing the sandwich he had packed that morning. Fat-free cream cheese with chopped green olives on wheatberry for her, PB & J for the kids.

"We've got a situation next door," Eric said. "You better meet the kids' school bus."

"What do you mean, 'a situation'?"

"Street blocked by a police car. Like that."

"On Azalea Court?" Bea scorned the dated architecture of the houses and regularly complained about the lack of closets. But she didn't mind the easy commute to the hospital or living mortgage-free in exchange for Eric's job as on-site manager, fix-it guy, and gardener. "Must be a mistake."

"The cops look pretty authentic." Eric heard the defensiveness in his voice. He wasn't sure how he had become the poster boy for small-town living, but his wife had that effect on him lately. Nothing seemed to be happening on the street out front, so Eric sank into his favorite chair at the living room window.

"I've got clinic this afternoon," she said. "Give me the bullet."

Eric ignored the doctor-speak. "Iris seems to have gone missing."

"What does Asher say? Don't you two drink tea and gossip every day?"

Eric let that pass too. "Not since last Sunday. Some days he doesn't feel so well. He's ninety-four, you know?" He didn't add that recently Asher wasn't himself, and it wasn't just about Iris being sick.

"Why all the cops?" Bea asked. "Do they think someone took her? Why would anyone kidnap a sick old lady?"

"I don't know. But yesterday Evelyn told me she was very worried about Iris."

"Evelyn?"

He couldn't decide if Bea refused to learn their neighbors' names out of disinterest or disdain. "Evelyn. The nurse in Number Three? Asher hasn't let her in to visit Iris for three days."

"Oh, the Nosy-Parker. What about the daughter?"

"I called Lexi a few minutes ago. She hasn't spoken to her mom in a week."

"Iris hasn't spoken a complete sentence in longer than that," Bea said. "She's gone loony."

Even though she hadn't done more than wave at their next-door neighbors in ages, Bea claimed anything health-related as her area of expertise. When they first moved in, Iris had been very friendly, offering advice about the best fish markets and local farm stands, but recently she stopped coming outside. A couple of weeks earlier, Asher told him that Iris had dementia, probably Alzheimer's. It's usually a slow disease, he'd said, but Iris had a fulminant case. Eric looked up the word in the medical dictionary on Bea's desk. Fulminant: occurring suddenly and with great intensity.

"Loony?" Eric asked. "Is that your professional opinion?" He heard voices out back and hurried to the window to watch a cop in Asher's yard. The cop surveyed the stone barbecue pit Asher had built to celebrate his retirement forty years earlier, then poked around in the poison ivy beyond the mowed grass.

"Ha." Bea said. "Aren't the cops searching for Iris?"

"I guess so. I can't tell what they're doing."

"What about our kids?" Bea's voice grew worried. "They could be in danger too."

"I doubt it's anything like that," Eric said. "But wait, a cop is coming to the front door. I'll call you later. Just to be safe, why don't you pick up the kids and take them back to work with you."

"But I—"

The doorbell rang. "Gotta go."

Bea's sigh came across loud and clear. "Okay. But listen to me, Eric. You stay away from Asher and his trouble. Far away."

A uniformed police officer was at the door. "Good morning, sir. Are you Eric Golden?"

Eric nodded.

"We're investigating a missing person report. Have you seen Mrs. Iris Blum this morning?"

"Not for a few days. What's going on?"

"We've just started gathering information," the cop said.

"I'd like to help look for her," Eric offered. "I'm sure other neighbors would too. What can we do?"

"The detectives will be here soon. They'll be around to talk with everyone and will let you know when you can help. For now, please stay in your home."

"Will do."

"One other thing," the cop said. "You're the caretaker of this place, right? Do you have a key to the empty unit, Number Five? I'd like to check it out, just to make sure Mrs. Blum isn't in there."

"Sure. I'll find the keys and meet you there in a few minutes."

Rummaging through the drawer for the master keys to Number Five, he glanced at the family photos on his desktop. This year, Marc wouldn't smile because of his braces, and Morgan went along in rare sibling solidarity. Bea looked great, as always. There were things about her he still loved, even when she made him feel small. Like the wild dancing thing she did with her fingers on a desk or the dinner table, a syncopated drumming.

She was doing that the first time Eric saw her, at his college roommate's wedding. He and Bea were seated at the singles table with the other friends and cousins who came without a partner, and he noticed her fingers before her face. He couldn't believe fingers could be that strong and smart and graceful. He fell in love with her hands and then with all of her. The first thing she said to him was, "You have the loveliest philtrum I've ever seen."

"Loveliest what?" he'd asked, and she traced the indentation from his nose to upper lip with her finger.

"It's cute," she said, before reaching into her silver sequined purse for a miniature bottle of hand disinfectant. She was studying to be a surgeon and he hoped that wouldn't ruin everything. When the phone rang again, Eric's first thought was that Bea was calling back to apologize. He grabbed the keys with one hand and the phone with the other.

It was Asher, and his voice was shaky. "Eric?"

"Are you okay? What's going on?"

Asher's answer was a sigh so loud Eric could have heard it without the phone. "I need to talk to you. I messed up. Come to the back door, and don't let the cops see you."

Eric had no experience with missing persons or cops. He was a gardener. Well, he had an MBA, but selling things had never agreed with him the way growing things did. Bea made buckets of money and was saving up for a fancier house. Meanwhile, he could plant bulbs in the fall, mow lawns, weed around the lupine, repair broken porch railings, and build the occasional planter for tomatoes on someone's back deck. Their kids were in school, but Eric was on call for stomachaches and bringing cupcakes to class on birthdays and riding the school bus on field trips. He spent a lot of time alone but was rarely lonely. That was partly because of Asher.

"Gotta let the cops into Number Five. I'll be there in ten minutes," he said. "Hang in there."

"Hurry," Asher whispered. "Please hurry."

ASHER BLUM

Asher paced back and forth across his study between the window and the wall holding the photo collage Lexi framed for their last wedding anniversary. Ten images of Iris and him, spread out over their six-plus decades together. His favorite photo was the oldest, shortly after they met at Brooklyn College. And the one taken the day they moved onto Azalea Court, the gray paint still glistening wet on the front porch. It was the day after their wedding and the day before he started his position at the state hospital. The latest image was already five years old. Why didn't they take photos anymore?

He glanced at the clock on his desk. How long would it take Eric to get here?

Eric was his only real friend, besides Iris. At first, Eric made him nervous. Actually, Asher didn't approve of him. In Asher's world, men went to work and their wives looked after the house and kids. Asher would sit in his leather recliner by the front window and watch Eric's progress through the flowerbeds, snapping the dead blooms off with a sharp twist of his wrist, dropping them into that canvas bag he wore like an apron, clomping around in orange plastic garden shoes. Orange is no color for a man. He wasn't crazy about Eric's garden philosophy either. Why bother working so hard on planting and weeding if the result is going to be just as messy as nature? Iris always pulled any weed that dared to poke through the cedar mulch and lined her beds with corrugated edging. Asher helped her unroll the stiff metal and press it into the soft earth with his weekend shoes.

But Iris liked Eric, and she was a sharp woman for all her soft ways. And once retired, Asher needed someone to talk to. Some people might think that after a career of talking he would like silence in retirement, but it didn't work out that way. Besides, most of his patients would just as soon he didn't talk so they didn't have to listen and could return uninterrupted to whatever stories spiraled in their heads.

He didn't love being retired, but the timing worked well for him, with the hospital transferring its final patients the week before his sixty-seventh birthday. He wasn't a man to sit around watching *Masterpiece Theater* reruns. He worked every day on his research, reviewing patient notes and revising his manuscript, and that kept his mind nimble and his attention engaged. After four decades of clinical work, he had a lot to say about treating the mentally ill, even if he sometimes doubted that he was right about any of it. That's why his working title for the book was "What We Thought We Knew," even though Iris declared it was a stupid title. No, he didn't love being retired, but he had been content, until his carefully erected life somehow spun out of control.

He and Iris had worked hard. That's what you did if you grew up during difficult times. You carried a responsibility to give something back to your people, your community. God knows there was no glory in the work he did, treating the people society labeled as nuts and locked away, but he did his best. These younger doctors seemed to feel they owe nothing except to their stockbrokers. Even Eric's wife. Asher heard she had good hands, but what satisfaction could a surgeon get reshaping noses to make women look less Jewish?

He was glad when Eric and Bea moved in next door and the condo association hired Eric to shovel snow and manage the grounds, although he still disapproved of Eric's wishy-washy way with the garden. Sometimes a man had to make difficult decisions.

As a physician, Asher was used to examining the evidence, considering the possible scenarios, making logical decisions, and then treating the situation. When everything changed with Iris a month earlier, he thought he handled it well. But maybe not, because now she was gone. She must have left very early. When he woke up this morning the coffeepot was cold. Iris, her pocketbook, and her favorite flannel-lined blue jacket with fur trim around the hood were gone. Her cell phone was on the kitchen counter—some kind of secret message that he couldn't decipher.

He tried to keep calm, but inside he was reeling. And he had to face facts: his take-charge methods might not be working so well in this new and dangerous situation. Iris was gone. Who knows what she might say or do? A cop was standing at his front door, waiting for detectives to arrive and take over the investigation. He needed someone to talk to and the best candidate was Eric. But how on Earth could he adequately explain things to a young man who had never faced Asher's challenges?

He probably couldn't, but he had to try.

ERIC GOLDEN

When Eric arrived at Number Five, the police officer was waiting at the empty bungalow. Eric unlocked the door and stood in the living room as the cop walked through the rooms calling for Iris and getting no answer.

"I did a deep clean last week," Eric said when the cop returned to the living room. "Even refinished the floors. The new owners arrive this afternoon." He looked worried. "Do you think their moving van will be able to get onto Azalea Court?"

The cop shrugged. "Depends on if we find Mrs. Blum."

"What happens next, with your search?"

"The detectives assigned to the case are on their way. They'll interview everyone and probably call in a canine unit."

"Can neighbors help look for her?" Eric followed the police officer to the front porch.

"Maybe after the canine search. Sometimes they'll bring in the other public safety folks, like the fire department. And a drone. You'll have to ask the detectives about a civilian search when they get here."

Eric locked the door of Number Five behind them.

"For now," the officer said, "please wait in your house. The detectives will be here soon. They'll need to interview everyone on the street."

Eric did plan to comply with the officer's instructions, after visiting Asher. But a different police officer stood at the front door of the Blum house, arguing with Lexi Blum. Lexi's face was deep red and she waved her arms wildly, so Eric decided to check on her before detouring to the back door as Asher had requested. As he crossed the small yard between their houses, Lexi saw him and burst into angry tears.

"He won't let me in," she fumed. "I want to see my father."

The officer kept one hand on the doorknob. "The detectives are on their way, and they'll need to talk to Dr. Blum first," he said to Eric. "As soon as they're finished with the interview, Ms. Blum can enter."

"It's my house," Lexi said. "My parents' house. I grew up here. You can't keep me out. My father needs me."

"The detectives will want to interview you also, Ms. Blum," he said, then turned to Eric. "And all the neighbors."

Eric put his arm around Lexi's shoulders. "It's chilly out here. Come wait in my house until they're ready for you."

"It's chilly and it's going to rain, and my mom is out there somewhere while these clowns sit around and talk." She turned to the cop. "Why aren't you people looking for her?"

"The canine unit always searches first," the cop explained. "Before a lot of people traipse over the ground, possibly disturbing evidence and adding their scents to confuse things. The dog and handler will be here soon."

Eric guided Lexi toward his house. "We'll sit by the window so we can keep track of what's happening."

She let Eric lead her into Number One.

"Tea?" He added water to the kettle without waiting for her answer.

Lexi sat by the window where she had a view of her parents' front steps. Eric took his time in the kitchen, giving her time to pull herself together. He'd figure out a way to get her some time alone with her father, before the detectives interviewed her. Poor woman. She must be worried sick about her mom. Today was the first time Eric noticed the vertical frown lines around Lexi's mouth and that her long braid was almost entirely gray.

He placed the mug of tea on the windowsill near Lexi and stood holding his cup.

"You want to talk?" he asked. "Or should I leave you alone?"

"Sit with me, please." She warmed her hands in the tea steam. "Thanks for calling me this morning. I can't believe my dad didn't let me know Mom was missing." She paused. "Well, I guess I can. He's been odder than usual, recently."

"Since your mother got sick?"

Lexi nodded. "I thought he was just worried about her. But now I'm not sure. What have you noticed, living next door?"

"Honestly, not much. I've hardly seen your mother in the past few weeks. Asher told me she has an aggressive kind of dementia. That she's very confused, and it's hard to carry on a conversation with her."

Lexi nodded again. "I asked her last week about Thanksgiving. She and I always cook a traditional turkey dinner for the three of us. She didn't seem to remember what Thanksgiving was." Lexi dug in her pocket for a tissue. "Then Dad got on the phone and suggested we skip the holiday this year. Next, he cancelled my coming to dinner that night. I often have Friday night dinner with them . . ." Her voice trailed off. "I mean, I used to. He's cancelled Shabbos dinner the past three weeks."

"Any idea where she might have gone, if she wandered off?"

Lexi shrugged. "Recently she's been fascinated by the old state hospital burial grounds. She asked me to walk there with her one day, about four weeks ago. It took forever with her cane and the uneven ground, but she persisted. Then she sat on the stone bench at the edge of the burial field. You know, the place where bodies of unclaimed patients are buried? She just stared, looking like she might cry. It was spooky."

"Has your mother seen a doctor, a neurologist?"

"My father says he's the only doc she needs."

Eric could just imagine what Bea would say about that. His wife wouldn't even write a script for an antibiotic if one of their kids had a screaming ear infection. Maybe things were different when Asher was in practice? Still, Lexi didn't need to hear his doubts, so he smiled.

"One thing is for sure," he said. "Asher Blum is one strong-willed guy."

DETECTIVE SANDRA McPHEE

From the moment she and her partner arrived on Azalea Court, Detective McPhee had a hunch something might be hinky about the missing person situation. For one thing, a neighbor called it in instead of the husband. The patrolman who responded to the 911 call told her that something was "off" about Dr. Blum. She supposed that anyone who worked at the state hospital for forty years had a right to be "off."

McPhee had never been on Azalea Court before that morning. Pretty place to live, she thought, like so many streets in their town. She knew the bigger neighborhood of houses, condos, and apartment buildings that had replaced the massive brick buildings of the state hospital. She also knew the old state hospital grounds. Like many kids who grew up in town, the closed-down campus was a favorite nighttime playground, the ultimate spooky house setting. McPhee and her friends had hung out there most summer weekends, bringing blankets and bottles, candles and joints. Looking back, she realized they rarely thought about the people who had lived in those collapsing buildings, never considered the shadowy ghosts who might be wandering the hallways.

The hospital grounds were very different now. Only five original buildings remained, repurposed as offices or renovated for apartments and condos. She was particularly nostalgic about the coach house, a once-favorite venue for high school parties, now gentrified and reborn as a landscape school. She had lost her virginity on the second floor, where her favorite scenes in the movie *The Cider House Rules* were filmed. She couldn't see the old building from Azalea Court, but she fondly whispered, "Princes of Maine, Kings of New England" to herself.

Before entering the Blum bungalow, the detectives got a report from the uniformed cop. They asked him to stay at the front door while they interviewed the husband.

Dr. Blum answered the door at their first knock and stepped back to let them enter the darkened living room. Heavy curtains were drawn, sketching the lines of the furniture in charcoal.

"I'm Detective McPhee." She offered her hand. "This is Detective Walsh. We'll be coordinating the search for your wife."

"What are you doing to find her?"

"May we sit down?" McPhee asked. Dr. Blum nodded and collapsed into a corduroy recliner. McPhee sat facing the husband across a small round table with a vase of dried flowers. Walsh sat near the kitchen, opening his notebook on his lap.

"We've issued a Silver Alert," McPhee said. "That's when a missing person is an elder. By law we have to notify Elder Services, and we've done that. We've also called in a canine unit to search the neighborhood."

Dr. Blum's face was blank, as if he didn't understand. "A dog," McPhee added. "They are first rate at finding people who have wandered off."

"Wandered off," Dr. Blum repeated.

McPhee and Walsh exchanged quick glances. "Is that what you think happened, sir?" she asked.

"I don't know," Dr. Blum said.

McPhee smiled at him, trying to convey her empathy and her patience. "I'm so sorry this is happening to you," she said. "Why don't we start at the beginning. When is the last time you saw your wife?"

ASHER BLUM

Asher ran his index finger across the shiny wood of the round table. Iris used teak oil to polish the surfaces. "You should be able to see yourself smile in the shine," she liked to say.

"Dr. Blum?" The detective's tone suggested this wasn't the first time she had asked the question. "When was the last time you saw your wife?"

"Last night," he said. Hadn't he already answered this question a hundred times? "I went to bed at ten, as usual. She was sitting right here in this chair, reading her book." He patted the arm of the chair. "I didn't hear her come to bed."

"Was her bed slept in?"

He hesitated, then admitted, "I'm not sure. I take a sleeping pill and sleep very soundly."

"And when you woke up?"

"At six she was gone. There was no coffee brewed, no oatmeal on the stove."

"Were you worried about her?" the detective asked.

Asher shook his head. "Not really. She likes to walk, so I thought she decided to go out before breakfast."

"Where does she like to walk?"

"She's eighty-eight years old," he said. "And needs a cane, so she mostly walks on the sidewalks of the Hospital Hill neighborhood." Why did he say that? Iris preferred the paths near the river, even though he tried to convince her it was safer walking on the sidewalks.

"We'll start looking there. What happened this morning when

your neighbor came over?" McPhee looked down at her notes. "Evelyn Turner?"

"She demanded to see Iris and I told her Iris wasn't home. She didn't believe me and strong-armed her way into my house. Like the Gestapo! When she saw that Iris wasn't here, she started yelling at me, accusing me of something. Heaven knows what."

"Evelyn called the police department. She said she was worried about Iris."

"She's a busybody, always sticking her nose in other people's business."

"Are you worried about your wife now, Dr. Blum?" The detective glanced down at her watch. "She's been away for at least six hours."

Asher looked down at his lap. He was worried, of course he was. But he couldn't begin to explain it all to these people. They were young. They wouldn't understand the history involved, the complexities.

"Tell me about Mrs. Blum." The detective's voice was gentler now. "Has she been worried about anything? Has she been upset or ill?"

He looked from the lady detective—clearly the one in charge—to the man and back to the lady. "My wife has dementia," he said. "It's a fulminant type, that leads to mental deterioration in months rather than years. She has been very confused in the past few weeks. So, yes. That has been very upsetting to her, to both of us."

"I'm so sorry to hear that," the detective said. "Who's her physician?"

"I am. I take care of her medical needs."

The two detectives exchanged glances. Then the lady asked, "She hasn't seen anyone else? For medications or examinations?"

Asher took a deep breath. "No need. I can write prescriptions. I take excellent care of her."

McPhee nodded. "Has anything else been bothering her recently, anything you're aware of?"

"No, not really. Just with the confusion, she sometimes gets years mixed up and thinks she's still in college, living in Brooklyn." He tried to laugh. "It's not unusual with dementia."

McPhee nodded again. "No, not unusual, but our job is to look at all the possibilities to help us find Mrs. Blum as soon as possible. Can you think of anyone who might have a reason to want to hurt your wife?"

Hurt Iris? Of course not. Asher shook his head. "She is kind to everyone. Everyone likes my Iris."

"What about you?" McPhee asked. "Can you think of anyone who might have a beef with you, want to hurt you through your wife?"

"Why would anyone want to hurt a harmless old man?"

McPhee smiled. "All those years you were treating patients at the state hospital, were there patients or families who felt unhappy with the care, or unsatisfied with the outcome?"

Asher responded with a wry smile. "Very few people are satisfied about the treatment of mental illness. There's so much we don't know about what causes these diseases and how to treat them. We do our best, and we do have some excellent outcomes, but many families are disappointed with the results."

The front door opened, and a uniformed officer motioned to the male detective, who got up to confer with him, and then turned to Asher.

"The canine unit is here, sir. We need an item that your wife wore recently. A blouse or nightgown would be perfect."

Asher walked into the bedroom and took Iris's lavender flowered nightgown from the hook behind the door. He buried his face in it for a few seconds before returning to the living room and handing it to the policeman.

"I'm feeling very tired," he told the detectives. "Might I be left alone to rest?"

Both detectives stood. "Of course. We'll have to bring you down to the station for a formal interview, but that can wait until later. For the time being the officer will be stationed on your porch in case there are any developments in the case. We'll be back with any news or updates."

She shook Asher's hand. "We'll do everything we can to find your wife."

When they were gone, finally gone, he pushed the recliner way back. He picked up Iris's knitting basket and cradled it in his lap. Outside, a mockingbird in the bare magnolia tree cycled through his repertoire. Asher closed his eyes and let his mind drift.

When he met Iris in December 1949, she and Harriet were sharing a Bunsen Burner. Their chemistry lab assistant was Asher's med school buddy, bedridden with the fever and deep cough that had swept Brooklyn College that semester, so Asher was filling in. It was late afternoon, and the university had removed every other light bulb to save money. Shadows danced along the long tile tables, shrinking and elongating between the burner flames.

He had walked up and down the rows of freshmen students, wondering if any of them had a clue about the correct laboratory procedures. He wasn't concentrating entirely on the experiment because of that girl in the front row, her coal black hair hanging dangerously close to the burner. That's what he told himself. That he was touching her hair to get it away from the flame.

"Dad?" Lexi stood in front of him. "You okay?"

Why was his daughter in the chem lab? He looked at her blank-faced. Eric was standing next to her.

"Eric called me," she said. "What happened to Mom?"

Of course, he thought, Eric would have called her. Everyone sticking their noses into his business. Still, it was good that Lexi was there. He nodded to Eric.

"Daddy?" Lexi kneeled on the floor next to his chair, like she used to as a little girl. She rested her head on the knitting basket. "They wouldn't let me in before, while the detectives were here. I was at Eric's house and we were waiting until we saw the cops leave." She paused. "We snuck in the back way. Did you know there's an officer stationed on the porch?"

"A big mess, Lexi." Her nickname still stuck on his tongue. Alexandra was such a pretty name and it had power and meaning in their family. So many Alexanders and Alexandras who never made it out of Europe. But Iris wanted to call their daughter something up to date. "Something modern," she said, so he gave in to the nickname.

"It's okay. We'll figure it out. Talk to me."

He wanted to, but he couldn't think of what to say.

"Don't you think I'm old enough to know what's going on?"

Asher tugged her graying braid and half-smiled. "Almost."

Lexi took his hand. "Dad, did Mom leave you? Why would she do that?"

"Enough." Asher stood up awkwardly, spilling the yarn onto the floor and pushing Lexi away. "Please. I need to lie down."

EVELYN TURNER

Staring out her front window, Evelyn drank the last inch of stone-cold coffee. She willed her hand to stop shaking and her thoughts to cease bouncing back and forth. From guilty to smug, they ricocheted. From *what have I done?* to *he got what he deserves.*

It was *her* phone call that started this mess, and she didn't regret that. Something just wasn't right at Number Two, and she wasn't a person to turn away from a problem. Plus, she had no use for Iris's stuck-up doctor husband. Arrogant doctors were the main reason she left hospital nursing to open her home care agency. Earlier that morning she had walked next door to see Iris, just to check up on her, and Dr. Blum refused to let her in. That was the third time he had turned her away in a month. She had pushed her way into the house and looked around, but no Iris.

The last time she and Iris had tea together, Iris mentioned that her husband had prescribed a new medication for her heart. Didn't the good doctor know that it was frowned upon, bordering on unethical, to prescribe meds for family members? The old guy shouldn't be prescribing drugs anymore in any case. Did he read the journals? Keep up with all the medical advances? Why would he pay to renew his license and malpractice insurance all these years? Something felt so deeply wrong she couldn't stand it. So finally, she called 911. Now a police car blocked the Court, but nothing seemed to be happening.

Evelyn couldn't just sit around and do nothing. It wasn't her nature, especially not now, when Iris could be hurt. Or worse. The only way she could think to help was to make a leaflet with a photo and some basic information. Then she and other neighbors could canvas the nearby streets and hand them out. Maybe someone had seen Iris. Luckily, Evelyn had pictures and biographical details stored on her computer, from the neighborhood directory she tried to get people interested in a couple of years back, a project that died for lack of participation. But Iris was a good soul, and she had sent Evelyn the information for her and Asher.

She put the empty mug in the sink and ran her index finger along the ragged edge of the newspaper clipping, circled in red marker, on the refrigerator door. She regularly clipped articles and recipes and ads and hung them on the fridge, using her collection of colorful food magnets—sushi and bagels and grapes and chocolate chip cookies looking good enough to eat. Donnie hated clutter and regularly took down the clippings, but he wouldn't dare remove this one. A grainy black and white photo of Old Main, looking pretty much the way it did when she was a student nurse at the state hospital, loomed above an italic invitation: *Join us Sunday, November 10, to dedicate the State Hospital Memorial Garden.*

November 10. Two days away.

"You're not going to that, are you?" Donnie kept asking.

Evelyn didn't answer. She didn't know.

"*So* not a good idea," he would mumble and leave the kitchen before she could respond.

Living in this *place* wasn't a good idea, she would say if she could talk about it, which she couldn't. Donnie was already living in Number Three when they met and fell in love and that was *before*, when Azalea Court was just a quaint little street bordering a state hospital.

Back then, she couldn't have imagined how the neighborhood would change around them. Sure, a few of the neighbors were the same, like Asher and Iris and their daughter, who moved out after college and visited less than a daughter should. And the couple in Number Six who had been there at least twenty years, but they didn't wave or say hello, and she didn't know them at all. Based on their Trump bumper stickers, she probably didn't want to know them, but she hated to think of herself as narrow-minded. There was even a homeless woman who parked her car near the Community Gardens, probably because of the portable toilet placed there during the growing season.

Yup, the feeling of the place had certainly changed. People didn't look out for each other like they used to. The erosion of the pulling-together feeling from the old days was another part of why she had been inspired to start her home care business, to take care of people. All that got her was a lot of bills and people calling her a Nosy-Parker. Maybe she *was* nosy, but only because she cared about her neighbors. And who was Ms. Parker, anyway?

She sat down at the computer and looked out the front window. She really should rake the leaves on the front walk. Eric did a pretty good job keeping the grass mowed and sidewalk cleared, but he couldn't keep up with the mass of leaves that fell and blew and collected each autumn. If she went out there, she might learn something about Iris. Or Asher might yell at her again, about minding her own business. It had been three hours since she called 911. Surely, they knew something by now. But if so, they weren't saying.

Her first task was to put something on the town Facebook page about Iris being missing. On the neighborhood listserv, too. Then, she'd make those leaflets and take them to everyone in the neighborhood. They would find Iris before something bad happened to her.

Searching for the files on her computer, she thought how much she wished she could live someplace else, anyplace else, but Donnie owned Number Three outright. With her business tanking they couldn't afford anything else on his wages, even with his weekend differential at the store. Donnie always praised his mother's financial smarts for buying the bungalow with weekly payroll deductions in the years the State Hospital was having a hard time keeping staff, pointing out that they wouldn't be able to buy anything in town these days. Evelyn cursed her mother-in-law's damn foresight.

When Evelyn had cut the dedication announcement from the Gazette and hung it on the refrigerator with a strawberry magnet, Donnie was upset with her. "That place has been closed down for twenty-six years. No, twenty-seven," he said. "I know you had a difficult time there, but even the ghosts have given up. Let it go, sweetheart."

She shook his voice out of her head. You couldn't just decide to forget. Memory persisted, at least this one did. What happened to her at that place was thirty-five years ago, but the ugly images whooshed back at unexpected times on a wind stinking of garlic, just as strong as if it happened last week.

That was the problem with living here: it was so close to bad memories. She could never escape them. But she could try to do a little bit of good in the world anyway. She could try to find a missing old woman, a kind soul who never hurt anyone.

She found the file with Iris's biographical information and opened it. It would be simple to make a leaflet and print enough copies to distribute. People on Azalea Court could rally together, take care of their own. Together, she and her neighbors would find Iris Blum.

GANDALF SIMON

It had been a decent-enough day. Gandalf saw the police car on the street but didn't think much of it. She sat at her desk, obsessively reading the national news in all its revolting drama, when the doorbell rang.

Her next-door neighbor Evelyn stood on the porch.

She handed Gandalf a piece of paper with a photograph. "Iris is missing. Have you seen her this morning?"

Gandalf looked down at the photo and shook her head. The picture was poorly printed, as if the toner was low. A gray streak bisected the woman's left eye and cheek, disappearing into her shirt. She could not remember the last time she saw Iris, but it could have been a week or two. Gandalf tended to keep to herself and stay in the house. But Iris had been the first person to welcome Jess and Gandalf to the Court when they moved in, almost five years before. She brought over a walnut-prune Bundt cake. "My mother's recipe," Iris had warned. "Don't eat too much at one time. Because of the prunes."

"She's missing." Evelyn waved her hand in the direction of the police car. "That's why the cops are here. I made these leaflets so we can look for her. Will you join our search?"

Under the photo, Evelyn had added a few biographical details. Name, address, age. For some reason, Evelyn had included Iris's birthplace: Storm Harbor, Maine. The sister island to the place where Gandalf had been imprisoned.

Those three small words—Storm Harbor, Maine—rocketed Gandalf back to Hurricane Island. To the horrible interrogation by federal security forces. To her escape, drenched and cold and lost and terrified. Walking a slippery, narrow path. Hugging a granite wall on one side with certain drowning in the quarry on the other. Needing to *get away get away get away*. Gandalf felt her body sway in wind and fear. A hand on her arm pulled her back to the present. She flinched.

Evelyn jerked her hand away. "Are you okay?"

Being kidnapped and imprisoned and interrogated on that wretched Maine island almost destroyed her. The fact that it was her government who did those things made it so much worse. Before that happened, she had considered herself a reasonably well-balanced and content person, confidant in her investigations and equations. She had trusted the scientific method with its beautiful logic to keep chaos at bay. After Hurricane Island she trusted no institution, no person. Except Jess, her partner, and to be honest she was not able to trust even Jess all the time. To save their relationship, Jess agreed to leave Manhattan. She got a teaching position at the nearby college and they moved to this circle of bungalows in the small New England city, dubbed Lesbianville, USA by the tabloids.

"I am fine," she told Evelyn.

But she wasn't fine. Not even close. From some things, people simply do not recover. Trauma, like what happened to her seven years, three months, and sixteen days earlier, changes a person at the cellular level.

"So, will you help us look for Iris?"

Gandalf nodded. Anything to get Evelyn out of her house.

Looking out the front window at the flashing cruiser lights after Evelyn left, Gandalf called Jess at the college and left a rambling voice message about the neighbor and the flyer and Hurricane Island. "Please come home," she ended the message. "I need you."

Gandalf leaned against the door jamb and squeezed her eyes closed. After her experience, how could she join the search for a missing woman?

How could she not?

ARNOLD NORTH

The neighbors didn't like him. That was okay because Arnold didn't like them either. Most of the people who lived on the Court, who lived in this whole damn town, were smug and self-congratulatory with their Commie politics and Bernie bumper stickers. It was much worse since the last election.

He and Aggie had as much right to live here as those people. They had both worked at the college for twenty years, Aggie mopping up the messes of snooty girls who never said thank you, and him keeping the air temperature perfect for their highnesses. They always expected that Aggie would quit when she got pregnant, but that didn't happen, so she kept working. He bet that their neighbors would just as soon they moved away, but their landlord worked at the college and rented them the house cheap. They didn't need friendly neighbors. He and Aggie kept to themselves, and they did just fine.

Just now, a nosy neighbor showed up at the door with a photograph of the old lady from in Number Two, the one with a flower name. Seems like she wandered off. He never cared for her old man, but she—Rose? Lily?—always had a smile and a hello and she sometimes gave him tulips or daffodils from her garden. The neighbor asked if he and Aggie would help look for her, if the cops said it was okay. Why weren't the cops out looking now? It wasn't that cold yet, but she was an old lady. Maybe they thought she'd wander on home or something?

After the nosy neighbor left, he told Aggie about the search party. They both had the day off before working the weekend, so maybe they would decide to join a search party. Even if the snobs on the Court probably didn't want their help.

GLORIA

Gloria didn't actually live on Azalea Court. She often parked her midnight-blue Subaru wagon just past the turn-off, on the gravel road serving the Community Gardens. Not all year, just for the eight months that the portable toilet was there for the use of the gardeners.

She couldn't park anywhere for too long at a time, but this was a good spot, one of her favorites. Out of the way. Nothing here but the gardens and the dog park. Pretty and safe. Sometimes the dog walkers tried to peer around the batik fabric she hung over the windows for privacy, but they couldn't see much and so far—knock on wood—no one had hassled her. She liked watching the same people walk by day after day. The old couple in their matching baseball caps with a logo she didn't recognize, the smiley redhead walking her dachshund, who had the most amazing collection of knit and embroidered doggy-coats Gloria had ever seen. Not that the dogs in her experience had much in the way of wardrobes. There was the guy with his walker from the Assisted Living facility down the road. He came by most days and always said, "Good Morning." When he didn't come, she missed him and worried about his health. Seeing familiar faces made her feel like part of the neighborhood, even though she wasn't, not really.

Some days, when her stomach wasn't churning with either hunger or worry, she pretended that she really did live there. In one of the pretty bungalows on the Court, not the pricey new houses in the development. She would consider the various units—this one's sweet paint job and that one's backyard with the fire pit. Then she would have to remind herself to Get a Grip. It didn't do to get too attached to a place, especially one that was totally out of her reach.

Today she saw a cop car on Azalea Court. Worrisome, but she couldn't afford to run down the battery using the car radio, so she didn't know what was happening. No matter the reason, police presence could be risky for her. She considered taking a drive. Maybe her friend in cohousing was home today and would let her take a shower. But she was curious. Even in a safe and privileged place like Azalea Court, life could turn so quickly. In the space of hours an ordinary life could become undone.

When Gloria came out of the portable toilet a few minutes later, rubbing her hands with sanitizer, a vaguely familiar woman with purple framed glasses stood in front of her car, holding a stack of papers.

"Good morning. My name is Evelyn and I live over there," she said, waving her arm, "on Azalea Court. Have you seen Iris Blum today?"

"Who?"

"Old woman. Wispy white hair and green eyes. Probably wearing a blue jacket. She's missing." She handed Gloria a leaflet with a large photograph.

"No," Gloria said, handing back the leaflet. "Haven't seen her. Sorry."

"Keep it. If you see her, please call 911 and let them know. We're worried that she's lost her way and can't get home. The police will be searching the whole area soon."

"Sure. If I see her."

"Thanks." Evelyn hesitated. "Iris has Alzheimer's and her family is very concerned."

Gloria nodded, but no way could she get involved. She might have to check with her cohousing friend or maybe take a drive. Police search parties poking around were never a good thing for someone like her.

DONNIE TURNER

From the kitchen window, Donnie watched the two detectives knock on Number One, wait for a minute, and then walk towards his porch. He had the door open before they could knock and invited them inside.

"I'm Donnie Turner." He flourished his arm in a mock courtly bow. "Your perfect informant. I've lived on this street my whole life."

The female cop shook his hand. "I'm Detective McPhee. This is Detective Walsh. May we talk with you for a few minutes about Iris Blum? You know that she's missing?"

"Yes, of course. Everyone knows everyone's business on Azalea Court. Especially my wife. Evelyn has already posted Iris's photo on Facebook and made leaflets. She's out now, distributing them around the neighborhood." Donnie handed a leaflet to each detective, not sure if he should feel proud of Evelyn's quick involvement, or if this would be another instance where people criticized her for getting too mixed up in other people's affairs.

"That was fast. When's the last time you saw Mrs. Blum?"

When had he seen her? Not for many days, for sure. Weeks, maybe. "She hasn't been outside much. Didn't put her flower garden to bed this year like she always does in October and November. My wife has gone over there several times—Evelyn is a nurse, and she's very fond of Iris—but Dr. Blum hasn't let Evelyn see her. Always says she's napping or something. That's why Evelyn called you folks this morning. She was so worried."

McPhee nodded. "We'll talk to Evelyn later. You said you've lived here your whole life? How long have the Blums lived next door?"

"They came in the early 1950s. That's when Dr. Blum started working at the state hospital. My mom worked there too, as an attendant. She and Mrs. Blum became good friends. Their daughter Lexi and I were born within weeks of each other in 1960. Our two families were pretty close until my parents divorced and then my mother died."

Donnie pictured his mother's photo albums with those curvy black corners that fell off when the glue died of old age. Family lore had it that he and Lexi, both only children, shared their childhoods like siblings. Black and white photos documented birthday cupcakes smeared across their faces and joyful splashing in backyard wading pools. He even used to be sweet on Lexi, decades ago, before he met Evelyn, but Lexi never seemed interested. He wondered about her sometimes, what her life was like now that she had left Azalea Court. She did something with landscape design, he thought. Seemed like she had turned into an odd duck.

"What can you tell us about Dr. Blum?"

Donnie laughed. "He's a shrink, what else do I need to say? He used to work long days at the state hospital. Always seemed head-in-the-clouds. I never understood the guy. He wasn't very friendly either, not like Iris."

"Do you have any idea where Mrs. Blum might have gone? Where she liked to walk when she went outside?"

"She used to love walking along the Mill River, but I don't know if she can still manage the hills. She never had a vegetable plot in the Community Gardens, but she used to help me weed mine from time to time. The last few years she sat on the bench and kept me company."

"We'll certainly check the river and the gardens," Detective McPhee said. "Any other thoughts about where Mrs. Blum might have gone? Or anyone who might have had difficulties or issues with her?"

Wow. Were the detectives thinking that someone hurt her, or kidnapped her? That put things in a whole other perspective. Should they all be worried? Donnie shivered.

"No," he said. "Everyone liked Iris."

FRIDAY AFTERNOON

What We Thought We Knew:

Table No 5. Shows the supposed Causes of Insanity in forty-four Cases· Intemperance 8, Masturbation 5, Disappointment in love 3, Pecuniary embarrassment 2, Hard study 2, Puerperal 2, Religious excitement 1

—Dr. WM Prince,
Northampton State Hospital Annual Report, 1858

THE WOMEN

We all had mixed-up feelings that afternoon as the detectives came around to our front doors asking questions, probing neighborhood history, poking around in our piles of dead leaves and moldy secrets. On the one hand Iris was one of us and we all worried about her, even those of us who had no use for her husband. On the other hand, well, no one likes police officers sticking their noses into their private business, right?

The detectives went door to door, skipping the cottages where no one answered and then doubling back later. Some of us welcomed them into our homes, having nothing to hide. Others were less hospitable. Not necessarily because of guilt. More often because of previous bad experiences with authority figures with guns, or perhaps just a suspicious personal bent. In any case, we were all invested in Iris being found quickly and unharmed. Both for her sake and so the peacefulness of our little enclave could return.

We did, however, begin to look at each other a little differently, even this early in the game. Wondering what that neighbor knew and wasn't saying. Or maybe *was* saying, and would it somehow implicate one of us in Iris's disappearance? What kind of gossip might be being spread? We all hated to be suspicious of our neighbors, but under the circumstances, can you blame us?

GANDALF SIMON

Gandalf paced. From the living room window through the small dining area and into the kitchen and then back, stopping each time to look outside for Jess. She watched the two detectives make their way from the Blum house to Number One, where no one answered the door, and then to Number Three. If only Jess would get home before they arrived at Number Four.

No such luck. When the doorbell rang, Gandalf considered pretending she wasn't at home. But despite everything that had happened to her, she still thought of herself as a person who followed the rules. She invited the detectives in and offered them chairs, then she perched on the arm of the sofa. It would be easier to jump up and leave the room if she had to. Sometimes she got anxious and had to lock herself in the bathroom for safety.

"I'm Detective Sandra McPhee," the female officer said.

Gandalf repeated her name silently and mentally filed it; it was important to keep track of the people with power, the people you might need to identify later.

"How can I help you?"

"You know that your neighbor Iris Blum is missing?"

Gandalf nodded.

"We're talking to all Mrs. Blum's neighbors," McPhee said. "Hoping to learn something that will help us find her. Did you know her well? We're trying to understand what kind of person she is."

"No," Gandalf said. "Not well at all. I moved here less than five years ago, and Mrs. Blum was already quite elderly. She brought us a cake, to welcome us to Azalea Court. Prune nut cake." Gandalf made a face. "Awful stuff, but she meant well."

"When did you last see her?"

Gandalf shook her head. "I have no idea. I have not had a conversation with her in months."

In fact, she could not remember the last conversation she had with any neighbor, more than a "Good Morning" when they happened to pick up their newspapers on the front stoop at the same time. She sat all day working at her desk trying to wrestle her research on hurricanes and decades of graduate school lectures into a book or at least a substantial monograph. Without much success, she had to admit. She had not been able to concentrate enough to clarify her thesis, and her thoughts usually spiraled inward doing no one any good. In any case, her study window faced the backyard, the tangle of shrubs and vines, yielding no useful information about neighbors.

"I'm sorry," she added.

"What about Dr. Blum? Any observations about him?"

Gandalf shook her head again. But there was one thing she remembered. One day soon after they moved in, Jess was at the college and the house felt too confining. She didn't have the energy for a walk, so she sat on the front porch feeling sorry for herself. She flushed, recalling that she had been crying in public and not even been aware of it. Mrs. Blum came over and asked what was wrong.

Gandalf had been so taken off-guard at the kindness in the old woman's face, at her question, that she told the old woman about what happened to her on Hurricane. "Trauma never goes away," the old woman said. Her husband still suffered nightmares from what happened to him as a child during the war in Europe. Should she tell the detective about that? It seemed so private, but maybe it had something to do with the old lady's disappearance.

"Mrs. Blum once told me that her husband still had bad dreams about his childhood during the war," Gandalf said. "In Europe. Probably not relevant, but I just thought about that conversation." Her voice trailed off.

The detectives stood up. "Thank you. That could be helpful. If you think of anything else, anything at all, please let us know. We'll come back later to talk to—" she looked down at her notebook and added, "Jess Simon. She lives here also?"

Gandalf nodded and closed the door behind them.

Had that been a good thing to share with the police? She couldn't decide. She wandered to her study and sat at her desk. Papers and folders were strewn over the surface, as if she were working on something big. Beyond the window, the wildly overgrown yard was equally messy and disorganized. Coming from a Manhattan apartment, she and Jess had no experience growing anything other than a potted amaryllis on a south-facing windowsill. She stood up, unable to face either the chaos of paper or the tangled mess of the yard.

She shut her study door behind her and sat on the sofa in the living room, staring through the window, waiting for Jess. She watched the Blum's daughter leave her parents' house and wander onto the green circle in the center of the Court, where she sat on a bench, shoulders slumped. Gandalf wished she were more like Jess, who would immediately go out there and offer her company, knowing that the woman must be frantic with worry about her mother.

Gandalf knew this about herself: she was not good with people. Especially with people in pain. When she was imprisoned on Hurricane Island, when she was the one hurting, she learned how comforting it is when people empathize. But she still found it difficult, impossible really, to express her feelings. She tried to project sympathy out the door and across the street toward Blum.

I'm sorry your mother is missing, she thought. But even her imagined voice was rusty and stiff, and she did not know how to lubricate it.

TIMOTHY BEAUJOLAIS

It wasn't the best day to move to Azalea Court, but they didn't have much choice. The moving truck had been scheduled weeks ago, and they needed to settle in before Winda's semester started in January. The college had been very welcoming to her. Hopefully this position would be worth leaving Brooklyn for, worth leaving his job and Imani's day care center.

Just their bad luck to have an emergency situation on their new street on moving day. Eric, the condo association caretaker, had called that morning to give them a heads-up that an elderly neighbor with Alzheimer's was missing. He warned them that cops were on the street and the moving van might have trouble getting in. Eric kindly left his number and said to call him when they were about an hour away. When Timothy had called just now, Eric said he had checked their house that morning, that everything was ready for their arrival. He promised to ask the police to move their cruisers to make room for the truck.

If necessary, they could probably crash at his twin brother's place nearby, but he would rather not for so many reasons. He and Jeremy had never been close. Their weird childhood could have forged a strong bond, but it didn't. When they went their own ways to college, Timothy had decided to leave all their family craziness behind. He majored in business and worked at becoming an ordinary guy. Jeremy drifted left and got all hot and bothered about climate change and plant species loss. Really, he was pretty embarrassing when he went around chanting the Latin names of extinct plants.

Winda liked Jeremy and encouraged Timothy to be kind. She said that moving back to his western Massachusetts roots would be good for Timothy, for their little family. The ancestors told her that, she said. They also told her that their new home was in a place with a lot of history and that their family had a role to play at the college and in the town. He tried to be open-minded about his wife talking to her ancestors, but what worked in Kenya didn't necessarily translate well to Northampton. Still, the job was a plum, especially for a first teaching position, and he was looking forward to being a full-time father for a few months while they settled in.

He crossed his fingers that the missing woman would be found, and his family could start their new life on Azalea Court with friendly neighbors welcoming them. Moving to a new town was hard enough. Moving to a mostly white town made it harder. Even with the help of Winda's ancestors, they definitely didn't need the bad karma of a missing old lady on their moving-in day.

AGGIE NORTH

People hated that she wore a hoodie, but it was none of their damn business. She wasn't a prejudiced person, but why was a hoodie any different from wearing a headscarf, and in this snowflake town everyone loved Muslims, right?

She wore it because she was bald. Not temporary chemo-bald. Forever-bald. Her hair started falling out in big clumps when she was twenty, shocking enough that her supervisor at work sent her to the college health service to check it out. The nurse practitioner called it alopecia. She explained that no one knew why it happened to some people, and there was no cure. Aggie's co-workers on the housekeeping staff were used to it, and no one there hassled her about wearing a hoodie.

Other people weren't so kind. The worst time was at Stop & Shop, right after that Black kid in Florida was shot, and the woman at the bakery counter called Security and two rent-a-cops brought her to their office for questioning. One of them held Aggie's hands behind her back, and the other pulled down her hood. He gasped and the other one let her hands go.

She had pulled her hoodie back in place. "You satisfied?" she snarled. "I'm bald. And I'm white. So, go to hell."

Aggie watched the progress of the detectives around the Court, thinking how much she didn't want to talk to any cops about anything. But like so many things in life, she didn't have any choice. When the doorbell rang she tried to rearrange her face into a less surly expression.

Really, it wasn't that bad. The detectives were polite and didn't ask about her hoodie. Since she didn't know anything about the missing woman or her husband, there wasn't much to talk about. Although that bothered her too, that she had lived here for so long and hardly knew their neighbors.

That was one of the reasons she and Arnie were saving their money to buy a farm. They needed to get out of this town and move somewhere people would be more like them—not bald, but *regular*—and there'd be fewer neighbors, in any case. So, they both worked hard at the college taking extra shifts when they could. They made birdhouses to sell at craft fairs. Arnie built them down in the basement and she painted them real pretty, with flowers and hearts. And she babysat, when she could find jobs.

Babysitting was how she had met Morgan and Marc in Number One. Their doctor mother was a class-A bitch, but Morgan was a sweet girl, even though her name was odd. Aggie asked her about it once, and she said she was named for a character in some old movie that her parents watched the night they got pregnant. How weird is that? In any case, bitch-mother never asked Aggie back to babysit after that first time. But Aggie heard that the people moving into Number Five next door had a baby, and she was hoping for some regular babysitting hours.

In the meantime, she stayed mostly in the house when she wasn't working. Arnie did the grocery shopping since that bad time at the store. She probably wouldn't join the search party for the old woman. She would like to help, but it wasn't worth the hassle. The sideways looks and the silent judgements. Not worth it, no way.

GLORIA

The yellow cat growled deep in her throat. Gloria dropped her book and pushed aside the thick fabric curtain to look outside. Two men walked past the car, talking loudly and letting their dogs run free. People using the dog park often ignored rules about leashes, so surprise canine visits, followed by their humans, were common. Thus, the benefit of a guard cat.

The cat had showed up three months earlier, making a nonstop racket until Gloria opened the car door and let her in. She hadn't planned to let the cat stay though. How could she, when she barely could feed herself? But the cat had looked up from devouring the crumbs of her turkey sandwich, leapt to the window, and made that warning growl in time for Gloria to turn off the radio and lie down under the blanket. She heard voices, but nobody bothered her.

"If you warn me when anyone's coming close," Gloria had told the cat, "you've got the job." She named her Canary. That night she discovered the pleasure of a small warm body tucked next to her chest in the sleeping bag. Gloria had never heard the cat meow, but learned her unique repertoire of sounds: contented chirps, rumbling purrs, and guttural growls of warning.

Gloria couldn't stop thinking about the missing woman. It was different than her own situation, of course, but it made her anxious to think about anyone wandering around lost, unable to go home or having nowhere to go. If the woman had dementia, would she have the sense to find a warm place to shelter, or would she freeze to death among last year's broken corn stalks?

How ironic to end a long and useful life in this place, where so many poor souls lived and died and were buried in unmarked graves because no one knew how to silence their screaming internal voices or calm their demons. She had once applied for a nursing position at the state hospital, and images from her tour still gave her bad dreams: communal toilet rooms without doors, a rack of housedresses in garish designs, a warning by the interviewer to always check the chair before sitting down, because some residents liked to empty their bladders in a pool on the plastic seat. When her mother forbid her to accept the job, she was relieved.

Now, sometimes she would walk the overgrown path by the river, its entrance mostly hidden by thick laurel bushes. An ancient weather-beaten sign announced in hand-drawn letters that this was Rebecca's Way. *Who was Rebecca,* Gloria often wondered, *and what happened to her?*

On sunny days if she felt especially safe, Gloria would leave the security of her car and sit on the new bench at the edge of the burial ground. She'd think about all the nameless patients interred there a century ago. Not only the ones who were mentally ill, but also the inconvenient people, the unwed mothers and disobedient wives, the homosexuals, the strange ones, the lost and homeless.

Like her.

If the state hospital were still open, she herself might be swept up and incarcerated. She could end up buried in that field.

DETECTIVE SANDRA McPHEE

Sitting in her car, Detective McPhee studied the list of the Azalea Court residents scribbled in her notebook.

#1 Eric Golden, Bea Kaufman, Marc, and Morgan
#2 Asher Blum, Iris Blum (Alexandra Blum)
#3 Evelyn Turner, Donald Turner
#4 Gandalf Simon, Jess Simon
#5 Family from Brooklyn moving in today, names?
#6 Arnold North, Aggie North

They had spoken with Mr. Blum, at least for the initial interview, and with Donnie Turner, Gandalf Simon, and Aggie North. The people moving in wouldn't know anyone, and the patrol officer already checked out their house, but that left more than half of the residents still to be interviewed, plus the missing woman's daughter. She reviewed the items on her mental to-do list as well: BOLO check, Silver Alert check, Elder Services check. The dog and handler were already out there sniffing around, and the drone team was waiting for her word. What was she missing?

It was her job to ask the questions and to listen—both to the answers and to what was not spoken. The neighbors appeared genuinely concerned about Mrs. Blum, even if a few of them might be too interested. But most missing person cases had someone like Evelyn, so eager to help that it triggered a little voice of suspicion.

This was the part of the job she liked best. Solving a puzzle, trying to figure out what was going on, and why. What made people do the things they did, even when they didn't really mean to or regretted it immediately afterwards? The other law enforcement stuff, the occasional car chases, and the rare shoot-outs that some of her colleagues loved, those weren't the important part. "You should have been a social worker, not a detective," her wife liked to say. But this was the right job for her. Raw and often ugly, but real. Her skills in puzzle-solving and reading people made her good at it.

Some people discount gut instinct, but professionals often rely on the combination of experience, following protocols with careful attention to detail, and simple intuition. Her wife was a nurse and she had it too, that finely-tuned sense born from years of seeing how things can look easy and fine on the surface and then go terribly wrong.

At this point, there was no solid evidence to suggest that someone had harmed Mrs. Blum. No evidence to suggest anything other than an elderly woman wandering off. Her cop sense told her that something else was going on, but it was early days yet. The husband was at the top of her list, but there was nothing solid there either. Just a rather pathetic old man with a shock of white hair fringing a bald head. A despot who acted like he still ruled over the land, even though his kingdom was an empty shell.

Next, she had to talk to the daughter, Alexandra Blum. It must have been quite an experience, growing up with Dr. Blum for a father.

LEXI BLUM

Lexi shivered and wrapped her scarf tighter around her neck. It was chilly on the bench in the small green center of Azalea Court, and the air smelled of rain. Clouds blew across the sky, hiding the sun. In better weather and nicer circumstances, the three benches would have made a nice place to hang out, if the people who lived on the Court had been more neighborly.

She had been fourteen when Iris proposed making this small park. Her mother's idea seemed as worthless and stupid as everything else that adults—especially her parents—suggested. Other people on the Court loved the idea though, and they chipped in for the benches and planted cheerful spring flowers—daffodils and tulips and iris. Nothing was blooming now though, not in mid-November. Not when her Iris-mama was missing. The plants wouldn't dare.

Lexi didn't have a plan, sitting there. She figured at some point pretty soon she'd have to go back to her father's house.

How had it already, in just a few hours, become her father's house?

She was deep in thought when the detectives joined her in the circle.

"I'm Detective Sandra McPhee," the woman said, offering her hand. "This is Detective Ralph Walsh. You are Alexandra Blum, right?"

"Lexi," she corrected. "Yes."

"We'd like to ask you some questions. Shall we go into your father's house?"

Damn. The detective also called it her *father's* house. Did that mean she suspected something awful had happened to Iris?

Lexi shook her head. "I'd rather not. Can we talk out here?"

The two detectives sat, McPhee directly across from her, and Walsh to the side with his notebook. Lexi wondered if this was a good cop-bad cop thing, or what. Too much TV, she decided, and besides, she hadn't done anything so why would they need a bad cop?

After getting Lexi's full name and address, McPhee asked if there were any other family members.

"Nope," Lexi said. "Just me. No siblings. No children. No relatives. My mother has some cousins in Maine, but my father apparently doesn't like them, or vice versa. I've never met them."

"Does anyone else live with you in your house?"

Lexi never knew how to respond when people asked that question. It was an oblique way of wanting to know who she sleeps with, and that was none of their business. In this case, the detectives probably needed to know who all the players were, especially if they suspected something ugly, but the question still pissed her off. Besides, there wasn't a simple answer. There was no category for people like her, who aren't particularly interested in intimacy with men or women. When people persisted in their questions, she told them that her sexual fantasies involved aliens. That shut them up good, but it was probably not a good answer to give a police detective trying to find your missing mother.

"I live in a communal house," Lexi told her. "Three other women. We also work together."

"What kind of work do you do?"

"We have a landscape design company, focusing on sustainable methods and native plants that encourage pollinators." She handed the detective a business card, although it seemed so irrelevant, so unrelated to this crisis. She was proud of the company she had built. She tried not to let it matter that her father had never respected her work, even when she got the graduate degree. When he wasn't around, her mother was delighted that Lexi loved to dig and plant as much as she did.

The detective put down her notebook and leaned slightly forward. "When was the last time you saw, or spoke with, your mother?"

Lexi flushed. Why didn't she come more often to see her mother? When her father canceled their Friday night dinner last week, she should have insisted. If only she hadn't been so self-involved.

"I haven't seen her in a couple of weeks," Lexi admitted. "My father discouraged me from coming over. He said her dementia was getting bad. I can't believe I listened to him and stayed away." She felt her throat swell and ache. "I spoke with her a week ago, and she didn't seem to remember what Thanksgiving is." She buried her face in her scarf, and the detective was quiet, giving her a few moments to compose herself.

When she looked up, ready to continue, McPhee's face had softened. "I'm sorry," she said. "This has got to be so difficult for you."

"What are you doing to find her?" Lexi asked. "It's awfully quiet around here."

McPhee nodded. "I know, but we're working. We've put out a Silver Alert, which is what we do for a missing elder. And a BOLO."

"What does that mean?"

"Be On the Look Out. The alert goes out across the Commonwealth so if, by some chance, your mother isn't still in the vicinity, other law enforcement departments will know we're looking for her. The canine unit is searching for her now, in the Hospital Hill neighborhood."

"Why there? Mom rarely walked over there. Too much cement, she said, and not enough trees."

The two detectives exchanged glances, and the guy walked out of hearing range and spoke into his phone.

"That's interesting," McPhee said. "Your father told us that she liked walking in the neighborhood, so that's where we started looking. Why do you think he said that?"

Uh oh. Was her father clueless about where Mom walked, or was he trying to sabotage the search? That didn't make sense. He must know that other people would tell the detectives the truth. Her confusion must have shown on her face, because McPhee looked at her intently and repeated her question. "Why do you think he would say that?"

Lexi shrugged, unsure why she needed to protect him, but unwilling to lie.

"Okay," McPhee said. "Tell me about your parents' relationship. Do you think they're happy together? Do they fight? Are you aware of either one of them being abusive toward the other?"

"No. No violence ever, that I'm aware of. They rarely argued, at least in front of me. But . . ." she hesitated.

"But what?"

"Dad was the important one in our family. He was the one with an influential position, the one who made every major family decision I can remember." When she thought about her parents, her father was in bold font to her mother's italic, in bright primary colors to her mother's muted pastels.

The detective hesitated, as if she wasn't sure about her next question. "Tell me about your father's childhood in Europe. Do you have a sense of how that affected him?"

Lexi was surprised that the detective knew about it, might think it was relevant. "What does that have to do with my mother being missing?" She heard the defensiveness in her voice and so did the detective. Lexi could tell by the way the cop leaned back slightly. The truth was, Lexi knew almost nothing about her father's early history. He refused to talk about it.

"Probably nothing," McPhee admitted. "We're just trying to understand your parents. If we know what makes them tick, we have a better chance of finding your mother. Do you think your mother was happy?"

"As far as I know," Lexi said. "Until recently, and then I'm not so sure."

"What happened to change things?"

"I don't know. But starting about a month ago, she seemed different. Troubled. That's when Dad diagnosed her dementia. It didn't make sense to me. My housemate's dad has Alzheimer's. She's read everything about it and goes on and on about how the disease progresses. It doesn't usually happen like this."

"What do you mean?"

"First of all, the change in my mother started too abruptly. One day she was herself and the next time I saw her she seemed confused, withdrawn. That's when my father started saying it wasn't a good time when I called or wanted to come over. I wish I had ignored him and come anyway. That's what I *should* have done."

The two detectives exchanged those glances again, and Lexi's eyes brimmed. She turned to McPhee. "What do you think happened to her? Did someone hurt her?"

"Can you think of anyone who would want to hurt her?" McPhee asked.

"No. But I haven't lived at home since I was a kid, and I don't know the new neighbors. Some of the newer people seem strange."

Lexi was thinking about the couple in Number Six, especially the odd woman who always wore a hoodie. But who was she to judge? People consider *her* an unnatural and strange woman—sixty years old, never married, and not interested in romance.

"This doesn't look good, does it?" Lexi said. Something bad must have happened, and her father might be involved, somehow. "This is so unlike my mother. She never wanted to be trouble to anyone."

Lexi covered her face with both hands and added, "I can't believe I'm already talking about her in the past tense."

IRIS BLUM

"Are you okay, ma'am?" The jogger and his German Shepherd regarded Iris, their heads tilted at identical angles. "Do you need help?"

Iris jerked back to the present. Had she been talking out loud? "Oh, no. I'm just fine."

"You sure you're okay?" he asked again. "I saw something on Facebook a few minutes ago about a lost woman. Said they were bringing dogs to this area to search for her."

"I'm fine," Iris repeated. "Thank you for asking. Guess I'd better get on home."

He nodded, and headed down the hill towards the river. Iris watched the dog bound across the burial ground. Was it disrespectful to let his dog run across the graves? She allowed herself a brief moment to wonder if Harriet was buried somewhere in that field with the other anonymous people in unmarked graves. She blew a kiss to the chilly air.

Leaning heavily on her walking stick to help her stand up from the stone bench, Iris tucked her pocketbook firmly under her arm and turned away from the river, away from the brown meadow. She felt unmoored, fuzzy-headed, passive. Those feelings were partly the shocks of the past few weeks, she figured, and partly her unhinged brain chemistry as Asher's pills slowly seeped from her body. Hopefully she'd be fully back to herself soon.

Search party and sniffer dogs? She'd better leave, but where should she go? She had no plan. How could she be so unprepared? She had to get word to Lexi that she was all right, to figure out a strategy for dealing with the facts she had learned, the impossible, unacceptable facts. How could she put things right, fix things that had gone so very wrong?

But first things first, and first was a bathroom, the portable toilet at the Community Gardens. With the help of her walking stick, she was quite certain she could make it.

MORGAN GOLDEN-KAUFMAN

Cop cars blocked the entrance to the street, so Mom dropped her and Marc off at the end of the road.

"Go right home," Mom said. "Your dad isn't answering his phone, but I'm sure he's there. Lock the doors and stay inside. You got your key, Marc?"

Marc rolled his eyes and tapped his chest where the key hung on a leather cord under his sweatshirt. He got out of the car and slammed the door before Morgan could scoot out his side. She would get her own key when she turned twelve in one year, seven months, and six days. She hated being dependent on her stupid, bossy brother.

People didn't lock doors much on Azalea Court. Dad locked theirs at night, but not during the day, especially since he was either home or working somewhere on the Court. So, it was surprising that they needed the key to get in, in broad daylight. Morgan figured it was because of the cop cars and Mrs. Blum being missing, which is why Mom picked them up at the bus stop and drove them home. Mom said that Dad wanted her to take Marc and her back to her hospital, but that didn't make any sense because of course they would be perfectly safe in their own house.

Marc went straight to his room and right away the battle noises blasted from his computer. Sometimes he played a cool world-building game, but mostly it was fights with aliens and other gory disgusting stuff. But Morgan couldn't really blame him. There were no other kids on the Court, only old people. Some afternoons they had soccer or art after school, but what were they supposed to do for fun on the other days? Ride their bikes by themselves? *Homework,* Mom said. *Be creative,* Dad said.

Mom and Dad had no idea that Marc played computer games for hours and she hung out with Aggie.

She could do homework, but she felt squirrelly sitting alone at the kitchen table with her math workbook. Creepy really, thinking about Mrs. Blum being missing and maybe hurt and maybe even dead. She liked Mrs. Blum and didn't really understand what it meant to have Alzheimer's and people thinking she had just wandered off, not knowing what she was doing.

She wrote Dad a note and left it on the kitchen table, held in place with the saltshaker. *Going for a short walk,* she wrote. *Home by dinnertime.* Her Dad would be angry. *What are you thinking going outside when there's a kidnapper in the neighborhood,* he would yell. She was only going across the Court to Aggie's but admitting that would be worse.

Aggie babysat for them once, when she and Marc were little. Usually Mrs. Blum would come over on the rare occasions when their parents went out together at night, but that one time she couldn't come. Mom was totally against having Aggie sit, but Dad teased that Aggie wouldn't corrupt their children's fragile political development in three hours. Marc spent the time in his room, but she sat and talked with Aggie who described her doll collection, and Morgan really wanted to see it. So, the next day she told Dad she was going over to Mrs. Blum's to help her roll knitting yarn into balls, and instead snuck over to Number Six. *Knock on the back door,* Aggie had said, *and I'll let you in if Arnie isn't home.*

Arnie didn't like her parents any more than they liked him, Morgan guessed.

She was too old to play with dolls, but you wouldn't believe Aggie's collection. Baby dolls, all of them. Aggie sewed clothes for them and hung the clothes on tiny hangers in a doll-sized wardrobe that Arnie made out of wood and Aggie painted with roses. The dolls had cradles and canopy beds with matching quilts and pillows. Sometimes when they played Aggie looked very sad and Morgan wanted to ask her what was wrong, but she was afraid Aggie might cry, so she never did.

Morgan's favorite doll was Cookie, and Aggie let her play with Cookie as much as she wanted. Cookie was the size of a real baby and you fed her water and she peed and you changed her diaper. Morgan had dolls at home, dolls of all different races and their privates looked almost real and they came with books about children in Africa and India and Peru, but none were as soft and cuddly as Cookie.

The day Mrs. Blum went missing, Morgan knocked on Aggie's back door. "Arnie is out doing errands," Aggie said. "But I don't know how long he'll be gone."

"That's okay. I can't stay long. Can I play with Cookie for a few minutes?"

Aggie opened the door and Morgan went to the extra bedroom, which was all decorated for a real baby but had dolls instead. She took Cookie from the crib and sat with her in the rocking chair. Two lullabies, she promised herself, and then she would go home.

ERIC GOLDEN

After leaving Asher's house, Eric couldn't bear the idea of sitting alone at home and worrying. He checked that none of the cops were around, then spent an hour in his backyard, cutting dead tree branches into fireplace-sized lengths. Not really part of the job, but his neighbors appreciated the gift of firewood as winter approached, and the tiring work was satisfying. When his muscles said *bastante*, he cleaned and put away the chopping shears, unlocked his front door, and tripped over two school backpacks.

What were the kids doing home? Bea was supposed to take them back to the hospital with her.

"Marc?" he yelled. "Morgan?"

He grabbed Morgan's note from the kitchen table and crumpled it in his hand. A *walk*? She went for a walk today? When there could be a kidnapper out there? What was she thinking? What was Bea thinking, leaving the kids on their own when there was danger on the street?

And Marc, how could the boy let his little sister go? He stormed up to Marc's room, following the booms of synthetic explosions and pushed open the door with more force than he should have. "You let your sister leave the house? Why didn't Mom keep you with her?"

Marc didn't take his eyes off the screen. "Dunno. Ask Mom yourself. Morgan didn't tell me her plans, so lay off."

"Any idea where she went?"

"Probably to Aggie's, as usual," Marc said, returning his full attention to the battle.

Aggie's? The hoodie woman from Number Six? What would Morgan be doing with *her*? How would she even know that woman? Just from the one time she babysat? Hurrying out of the house, he met Morgan running up the front steps.

"Where were you?" he yelled, feeling both furious and relieved. "And don't lie to me."

ASHER BLUM

Despite his exhaustion, Asher couldn't nap, no matter how many sheep he counted. He dragged himself out of bed and found some yogurt in the refrigerator. Iris's voice was stern in his head, telling him how unhealthy it was to add chocolate syrup to yogurt, so he didn't. Carrying the bowl to the front window, he felt virtuous for the first time in weeks.

Opening the curtains enough to see the green center of Azalea Court—he thought of it as Iris's Circle—he watched Lexi talking with the two detectives, wishing he could hear their conversation. The male detective, the quiet one, not the boss, stood up and turned his back to Lexi. He talked on his phone for a couple of minutes, waving his free hand in the air. Then Lexi got up too and started walking slowly towards his house. Her face was red and puffy.

He put the bowl of unfinished yogurt in the sink, wondering for a moment if Iris would be home to clean up the kitchen like she always did. He sat in Iris's chair and hugged her knitting basket. He hoped Lexi wasn't going to cry. He couldn't stand watching her cry. When she was little and cried, he simply left the room and let Iris take care of it.

He listened to the murmur of voices on the porch. How could his life have come to this? People being logged in to enter his home. It was inexcusable. Indefensible. After everything he had given to this community. But not a huge surprise, perhaps. For years he had waited in vain for people to acknowledge his contributions to the state hospital and the town in a tangible way. There was Prince Street, and Earle Street, but no Blum Street. Even the Haskell Building was named for a colleague who had been a decent physician, but why should *she* be honored that way and not him? Was it anti-Semitism? Whatever the reason, his four decades of service were largely unappreciated.

He cradled his head in his hands, elbows resting on Iris's yarn basket with the half-finished gray cardigan she was knitting for him on top. Try as he might, he would never understand people. That was a peculiar thing for a psychiatrist to admit.

"Dad?"

Lexi stood in the doorway. Her face was more composed now, tears wiped from her eyes. She walked to his chair and leaned over for a hug. They didn't hug much in their family. He held her as long as he could without seeming pathetic.

"Sit with me," he said.

Lexi sat and took his hand. "I love you, Dad."

Anything else would have been fine. If she had asked how he was, or where he thought Iris had gone, or what on earth the detectives were doing, he could have handled it. Even if she yelled at him, blamed him. But this? He felt his throat swell and ache and then he couldn't stop the sobs.

DONNIE TURNER

It was hard to stay inside with nothing to do except watch the comings and goings of the detectives moving around the Court. He wanted to help search for Iris. He needed to check on Evelyn, who was wandering around the neighborhood with her leaflets. She had been so emotional recently, with all the talk about the state hospital, the plans to honor the ugly past with benches and gardens. Why couldn't people just let the past go?

He had never entirely understood Evelyn's obsession with the state hospital and with the guy who assaulted her. Sure, it was traumatic, horrible, but it was a long time ago. And now she had *him*, loving her and taking care of her.

Maybe he wasn't being fair. Or maybe he just didn't get it, because his decades-old memories of this place were mostly good ones. All the kid stuff that showed up as black and white images in his dreams. How strange was that, that most of his dreams were in color, but the ones from childhood—from growing up on Azalea Court, playing every day with Lexi—those were in black and white. Those scenes replayed frequently in his head, especially the ones where he and Lexi tried to rig up a way to cross the Mill River using the old cable. They never managed anything other than sending notes and small objects in a tin bucket, but they sure had big ideas about it. The adventure that never showed up in those mental newsreels was the time he and Lexi were about ten—how could that be fifty-five years ago?—and they tried to find an entrance to the underground tunnels rumored to link all the hospital buildings. He tried not to think about *that* night.

Sure, he had his own ghosts, but Evelyn was totally mental about the place. She considered not marrying him when she learned they would have to live on the Court. He wished they could move, but his salary from the hardware store wouldn't buy a closet in the Northampton housing market. Evelyn had moved into the cottage when she was twenty-four and never grew comfortable living on the Court. But it got worse when her home care agency started to fail, and she was around all day. Maybe her business would pick up again, and they could look for a place to live in a less expensive town nearby.

The detectives weren't in sight anymore. He wondered which house they were in. A stranger with a German Shepherd on a leash stood in the circle, looking around. Donnie grabbed his jacket and hurried outside.

"Is this where the missing woman lives?" the stranger asked.

Donnie pointed to Number Two.

"There was a notice and photo on Facebook," the man said. "I think maybe I saw her."

"Where? My wife posted that."

"Sitting on the memorial bench at the top of the burial field. You know, the dog park?" He pointed vaguely west.

"Was she okay?" Donnie asked.

The man shrugged. "Guess so." He hesitated. "Though I think she was talking to herself."

"Let me find the detectives. They'll want to interview you."

The man shook his head. "I don't want to get involved. Just tell them I saw her there."

"Sure. But did you see anyone else around?" Donnie asked, channeling all the cop shows Evelyn liked to watch on television.

"Someone wearing a hooded sweatshirt was in the field," the man said. "Not sure if it was a man or woman."

"That could be important," Donnie said. "I'll find Detective McPhee for you."

The man tugged the dog's leash and turned to leave, muttering about not sticking his nose into other people's business.

Donnie hurried to the policeman on the porch of Number Two. By the time he turned to point to the man and his dog, they were out of sight.

"Where are the detectives?" Donnie asked.

The patrolman pointed to Number One.

"I need to talk to them."

"I'll let Detective McPhee know," the cop said. "Do you want to give me a message?"

Donnie hesitated. He would rather tell her himself, but time might be important. "Just tell her that a guy with a German Shepherd was here. He said he saw Iris at the burial ground just now and she was talking to herself. Lots of people do that, right? Otherwise she seemed fine. Oh, and that he saw a person with a hooded sweatshirt walking nearby, but no one else."

"Thanks. I'll tell her."

"Um. One more thing," Donnie said. "Since you guys don't live on Azalea Court, you might not know that one of our neighbors always wears a hoodie. Aggie, from Number Six. Probably just a coincidence, but still."

JESS SIMON

Jess didn't hear Gandalf's message until after her Resistance Lit class, and then it took ten minutes before she could break away from the three students arguing about whether or not *Mudbound* was an example of cultural appropriation. The students were smart and passionate, and it was an important question, one she normally would have followed to the student union and continued over coffee. But seeing the missed call notification flash across the phone screen was ominous.

The first disturbing thing was that Gandalf never called during the workday. The second was the message itself. It was panicky, almost incoherent. Something about a missing neighbor and dementia and danger and police blocking the Court. And Hurricane Island.

The Hurricane Island part was what scared Jess most. Her beloved had never been the same since she was kidnapped and taken to that awful, awful place. Gandalf had tried putting it behind her, tried going back to her work, but she couldn't concentrate and finally accepted a severance package. Getting out of Manhattan seemed important, and Jess's new job at the local college provided the perfect safe and comfortable place to live. Gandalf insisted that she understood about PTSD but refused to see a therapist. Hopefully, she would be able to get to work on her book soon; science had always been Gandalf's passion and it might be her therapy. But in the meantime, Jess worried about her. The phone message was disjointed and alarming enough to send her hurrying home in the middle of the afternoon.

The police cars weren't blocking anything on the Court when Jess got there, but a moving van was unloading at Number Five. No one was in sight except the movers carrying a crib with painted giraffes up the

stairs. Normally, Jess would have gone over and introduced herself—
she would later—but first, she had to make sure Gandalf was okay.

Well, maybe not okay, but okay enough. Maybe she should suggest
that they go away for the weekend, insist on it. They could probably get
a room in their favorite B&B in Provincetown. If only she could protect
Gandalf from the past, and from what might come in the future.

TIMOTHY BEAUJOLAIS

Timothy looked out the front window of Number Five. He swayed back and forth, singing the Zulu lullaby Winda had taught him, hoping Imani would consent to nap in the Bjorn since her crib wasn't assembled yet. *"Thula thul, thula baba, thula sana."* He sang softly, so Winda wouldn't make fun of his pronunciation.

"I hear you," Winda called from the kitchen, where she was unpacking the boxes labeled KITCHEN ESSENTIALS. "Nice singing!"

His luck at finding Winda, and her loving him, never ceased to amaze him. Before Winda, all his friends had been white, even though he and his twin brother were biracial. It had been pure luck, his being randomly paired with Winda for a project in their global economy graduate course. Especially lucky since Winda wasn't interested in economics. She claimed she signed up for the class to round out her knowledge of the experience of African immigrants. But once she and Timothy were assigned to work together, Winda understood that she was sent by her ancestors to get him in touch with his roots. He figured he owed her ancestors big time.

He still didn't totally get what Winda meant by the "ancestors." They weren't really ghosts, she explained, but they spoke to her and she listened. Ghosts or not, Winda and Imani were the best part of his life, almost making up for his crazy-ass childhood and lonely college years. He still found it hard to believe that Winda gave up her plan to return to Nairobi so she could stay in the US with him, despite all the immigration hoops and hassles.

He watched as the woman next door at Number Four slammed her car door and rushed into her house. Then he admired the green area circle with benches and flowers. He wondered if they ever had barbecues or potlucks and whether or not this odd little enclave would welcome his family.

"*Thula thula thula baba*," he ended the song with a whisper. "*Thula thula thula sana*." Imani was asleep. He wandered into the kitchen, proud of his papa expertise, and stood next to Winda. She paused in her unwrapping of coffee mugs, and they looked down at their daughter.

The doorbell rang. Imani startled and whimpered.

"You keep singing," Winda said. "I'll get the door."

He started the song again and followed Winda to the doorway to see their first visitor, a person wearing a long denim skirt and hooded sweatshirt which covered her head and shadowed her face.

The person at the door stared at Winda and didn't speak for a few long seconds. Then she said, "I'm Aggie. I live at Number Six. Next door." She hesitated and swallowed hard. "I babysit and heard you have a child, and I wondered if you needed a sitter."

Winda smiled. "I don't know yet. We just got here. But come in. I'm Winda, and that's my husband Timothy and our daughter Imani." She turned to Timothy, who waved, still swaying with the baby. Imani's eyes were open and she stared at their guest.

Aggie stared back at the baby. She swallowed hard, then blurted, "I've never babysat for a—Sorry." She turned away and fled down the porch stairs, across the brown grass and into her house.

Winda took Timothy's hand.

AGGIE NORTH

She had no idea the new neighbors were Black. How could she know?
The furniture being unloaded looked regular, like any family's. She
wasn't prejudiced, but her mama always insisted that people were
happiest when they kept to their own kind. Still, Aggie really needed
babysitting hours and dollars, and that baby looked very sweet. Didn't
matter anyway, since by freaking out and running away like that she
had totally screwed up any chance of getting to babysit for them.

She was shook up by the visit next door, so she went into the doll
room. Cookie was in the rocking chair where Morgan left her. Aggie put a sky-blue sweater over the doll's dress—it was chilly in the
house—and cradled Cookie in her arms and rocked her to sleep.

GLORIA

Two things happened at once. Canary growled deep and guttural, and someone knocked on the driver's side window.

Gloria used the small peek-hole in the cardboard. It was an old woman with flyaway white hair, just like the picture on the leaflet. The missing woman with Alzheimer's. Gloria shook her head, her brain jumping ahead to the potential consequences of getting involved with this woman, no doubt the subject of a police search right now.

Such a bad idea.

Canary growled again. This time it sounded accusing rather than warning. *How could you not at least talk to her,* the cat seemed to be saying. *You're not the only person with problems.*

"If I get in trouble," Gloria said to the cat, "it's going to be your fault. You know that, right?"

The woman knocked again.

Gloria opened the front door and peered out. "What do you want?"

"My name is Iris," the old woman spoke quickly. "May I come in?"

"People are looking for you," Gloria said. "Why?"

"I ran away from home. From my husband. Please help me."

Gloria held her breath. How could she turn this woman away? "Get in," she said.

Iris settled herself in the passenger seat, shaking. Gloria couldn't tell if she was shivering or trembling. "Are you cold?" Without waiting for her answer, Gloria transferred the cat to Iris's lap and pulled a comforter from the back seat. Tucking it around Iris's shoulders, she asked, "What do you need?"

"To get away from here," she said. "I heard that they're looking for me with dogs."

"Where do you want to go?"

"It doesn't matter. Just away from here, at least until the dogs are gone."

Gloria rubbed her face with both hands. This was *such* a bad idea. What would the cops do if they thought a homeless woman was hiding an old lady who was missing, who ran away from a husband? The woman didn't look abused but you couldn't always tell. The cops would probably accuse her of kidnapping, or worse. Gloria looked at Iris, trying to weigh options, trying not to think about her own mother, about the kind people who had helped their family when her parents were old and sick. That was different, wasn't it?

"I don't know," Gloria said. "That's not a good idea for me."

"Please," Iris said. "I have money. I can pay." She opened her pocketbook to display a thick stack of twenties in a nest of pill bottles, a comb, and a clear bag with shampoo, toothpaste, and toothbrush. Canary's head disappeared into the bag.

Gloria glanced at the jumble of pill bottles. "Are you sick?"

"No. I'm fine. I'll explain once we're away from here. I don't want them to find me and take me back."

Canary jumped off Iris's lap and snarled her deep-throat warning.

"Oh," Gloria said, looking out. "Two cops heading this way." She turned to Iris. "You've got to get onto the floor, quickly, and I'll cover you up."

"I'm eighty-eight years old. I don't move quickly," Iris said. But she slid off the seat and curled up on the floor. Gloria covered her with the comforter and put the cat on top. "Stay there, Canary."

When the cops knocked on the driver's side window, Gloria pulled aside the fabric and rolled it down.

"We're looking for this woman," the policewoman said, handing Gloria a photocopied picture of Iris. "She was seen around here about an hour ago. She has dementia and wandered off from her home. Have you seen her?"

"No, but I just got here myself a few minutes ago." Gloria handed the paper back. "I'll sure keep my eyes open for her."

When the cops were gone, Gloria spoke to the comforter on the floor. "Okay. You stay down there, and we'll take a little drive. Get you away from cops and dogs. Then we can figure out what to do next."

DETECTIVE McPHEE

McPhee considered the patrolman's news. Iris being spotted at the burial ground could be the break they needed, and McPhee was grateful, even if it came from Facebook rather than police work. She had radioed the canine team with the news that Mrs. Blum was sighted at the memorial bench overlooking the burial ground. The dog was still sniffing his way along the Mill River, but they'd head over to the bench. A couple of foot patrolmen were already dispatched to the spot. She called the station requesting the drone flight right away, before the rain started. A quick look now with the infrared camera when they'd had a sighting might just do the trick.

She turned to her partner. "Probably a good time to talk to the guy we missed in Number One, the caretaker. What's his name?"

Walsh checked his notebook. "Eric Golden. Wife is Bea Kaufman. Two kids."

Ten minutes later, McPhee and Walsh sat in the living room at Number One Azalea Court.

"Can I get you tea?" Eric asked. "It's raw out there."

"No. Thank you, Mr. Golden," McPhee said. "Before we start, are your children at home?"

He looked surprised. "Call me Eric," he said. "They are, but the kids wouldn't know anything."

McPhee shrugged. "Probably not, but it's worth asking. If that's okay with you."

It was always worth talking to children and old people. They tended to be more observant than busy adults, plus people often barely noticed kids, and talked in front of them as if they weren't there.

The children must have been listening in the hallway. When Eric called, they entered the room quickly, stood in front of the television, and stared at McPhee.

"I'm Detective McPhee," she said. "What are your names?"

"I'm Marc."

"I'm Morgan."

"Thanks for helping us out," McPhee said. "Have either one of you seen your neighbor Mrs. Blum today?"

Both children shook their heads. "Our mom drove us home from school," Marc offered. "Dad was worried the school bus wouldn't get through or something. I came right in and went to my room. Unlike her!" He pointed to his sister.

"Yeah, you went right to your computer and started killing people," Morgan said, then slapped her hand over her mouth as if she realized what she said. "You don't think Iris has been killed, do you?" she asked McPhee.

"We have no reason to believe anyone hurt Mrs. Blum," McPhee said. "Where did you go after school, Morgan?"

Morgan glanced at her father before answering. "I visited Aggie. I like to play with her dolls. I know I'm too old, but her dolls are wicked cute. I didn't see anyone except Aggie." She stopped to catch her breath. "I want to be a detective when I grow up."

McPhee smiled. "Have either one of you noticed anything unusual lately, with Mrs. Blum?"

Morgan and Marc shook their heads, their faces serious and eyes wide.

"Thank you. If you think of anything else, please ask your father to let me know." She nodded to Eric, who sent the kids off to do homework.

She turned to Eric. "You know the Blums pretty well, don't you?"

"I guess so. Asher more than Iris."

"Tell me about Asher Blum," she said.

He rubbed his upper lip. Then he pulled his hand from his lip, looked at it, and grimaced. McPhee stared at him and he laughed.

"Did you know that indented place under your nose has a name? Philtrum. When we first met, my wife thought it was cute, the way I rub it, but now she says it's unsanitary and I'm trying to stop." He paused and looked from one detective to the other. "Sorry. Guess I'm upset about Iris. What kind of things do you want to know?"

Hmmm, McPhee thought. *He's nervous about something. More likely something about that wife of his, rather than the case. But you never know.*

"Whatever you can think of," she said. "What kind of man is he? How did he treat his wife? Did you ever notice problems between Mr. and Mrs. Blum?"

"It took Asher and me a long time to become friends. Different generations, you know. He could be my grandfather. We don't really share personal details."

She nodded. "What about recently? Have you noticed him acting differently?"

"Asher hasn't been himself the past month or so," Eric said. "His wife has Alzheimer's, so it's not surprising he's been upset. He takes really good care of her."

"Anything else you can think of?"

Eric hesitated again. McPhee recognized his silent inner debate about whether to share something with the authorities. Something that could possibly reflect badly on a friend. She wondered how this man would resolve the dilemma.

"No," he said. "Nothing else."

LEXI BLUM

Her father's weeping undid her. Lexi couldn't remember ever seeing either of her parents cry. When his sobs subsided into hiccups, she got him a glass of water. He drank it quickly and left the living room without speaking. She wanted to follow him and demand that he talk to her, but she didn't. That wasn't how their family operated, even in a crisis. Of course, they'd never had a crisis anything like this before. Instead, she opened the heavy curtains her mom insisted be closed to protect the upholstered furniture. It was just as dark outside, with dusk coming and the rain on their doorstep.

Maybe you never get to understand your parents' marriage. If she had a sibling and could have observed her parents interact with another kid, perhaps she would have more insight into what made their more than sixty years together work. Seemed like it mostly *did* work for them, even without the benefit of her understanding, at least until very recently. Now with her mother missing it felt critical to figure out something about their marriage that would help Lexi find her.

Lexi's relationship with her parents had always been perplexing. For one thing, they would never tell her about when they were young, no matter how many times she asked. She could understand that more with her dad. He grew up in Europe during the war and lost most of his family to the Nazis. Maybe that's what made him so secretive and opaque, even when it didn't make sense. Like with her name. It was old-fashioned and formal, and she had asked over and over where it came from. Her mother said, "Ask your father," but he wouldn't say. Finally, he told Lexi she was named for all the Alexanders and Alexandras who were gone, killed in eastern Europe.

"But which one, most of all?" she asked, wanting a face and a story. He wouldn't say any more.

As far as she knew, her mother didn't have a good reason to be secretive about her childhood. When Lexi was a girl she begged to visit the island where her mom grew up. Islands were romantic, at least in books like *Anne of Green Gables*. Mom said her island family didn't like Asher and they'd never go back there. As Lexi grew up, she wished her mother was different, that she had a career or something important to do with her days. She knew the importance of context, and that women had fewer options in the 1950s. But Lexi always hated the way her mom looked to her husband for validation, expecting him to make all the important decisions affecting their family.

They wouldn't talk about being Jewish either. Did that have something to do with the Nazis too, and fear? Her mother made challah and lit candles on Friday evenings but never attended a synagogue. Matzoh at Passover and the menorah at Hanukkah, but no God. No one would answer Lexi's questions about religion either. Sometimes Lexi wondered what the three of them had discussed at the dinner table all those years, and she couldn't remember any of it.

After she found that old photo of that woman with her mother, Lexi had spent hours fantasizing about Harriet. Dad said Harriet led Mom into danger, so maybe Harriet was an independent woman. Maybe she was a leader, not interested in following a man. What would it have been like to have Harriet as her mother? Lexi asked her mom about Harriet one time, obliquely, on a visit home her freshman year of college. She was feeling lonely at school, hadn't made any good friends. She and her mom were in the kitchen. Mom was making her own mother's prune nut cake recipe and Lexi was pretending to read a book at the table.

"Mom," she asked, "who was your best friend, growing up?"

Mom's face lit up. "Harriet." Her lips smiled around the syllables of the name. "We grew up together in Maine."

"Tell me about her?"

Then just as quickly, the light went out, and her mother looked down at the dark brown cake batter and started beating. "Nothing to tell. We lost track of each other years ago."

Now Lexi *had* to talk to her father, had to understand what was happening in the family. She called out to him but there was no answer. Walking down the hallway, she saw a sliver of light under the door of his study. She hesitated, then opened the door. Asher was at his paper-and-book-strewn desk, hunched over a large green notebook holding his old-fashioned fountain pen, the kind you have to fill from a bottle of ink.

"What are you doing?" she asked.

"Working on my book," he said without looking up. "You know, Pliny Earle was a fascinating man, way ahead of his time. Other nineteenth century psychiatrists were claiming they could cure insanity, but he faced the truth. Even more amazing, he wrote the truth."

Lexi wanted to scream. Or shake him. Moments ago, he was weeping into his missing wife's knitting basket and now he's writing? How could he even be thinking about a shrink who died over a hundred years ago when his wife could be in awful danger right now, and maybe it was his fault? How could he talk about facing the truth when he'd been hiding it for decades? Whatever it was.

She felt her cheeks begin to burn with anger. There wasn't even an extra chair in his study, no place for her mom to sit with him and discuss his work. No place for her either. Fuming, she pushed a pile of papers from his desk onto the floor and sat on his desk.

"Forget Pliny Earle. Talk about our family."

He watched clouds of fury gather on Alexandra's face. She looked ready to erupt, to scream. Looking down at his lap, he forced himself to leave the papers scattered on the floor. He could understand his daughter being so angry, and he couldn't begin to defend himself, but he was drowning in memories and regrets. With his only offspring glowering at him, snapshot moments tumbled over each other, memories drenched in joy and sorrow, in a wild waltz of angry words and loving ones. Iris had always hated how at moments of sorrow he disappeared into his brain, leaving her alone and uncomforted. He felt himself deserting Lexi now, but was unable to stop himself.

Images of hiding in the woods with partisans danced the hora with memories of his daughter's birth and his deep joy. Shame about things he did in his life merged with the babies Iris lost, the pain that carved deep worry lines around his sweet wife's eyes.

Without thinking, he hummed a few verses of the wordless lullaby his sister had sung to him eons ago. By the time he realized what he was doing, it was too late, and the old memories enveloped him. Iris and his work had mostly banished those demons. When they came, rarely, usually triggered by a snippet of song or the smell of pine forest, he couldn't resist them. Within seconds he tumbled back into the war, hidden with his brother and sister deep in the forest, while their parents fought with the partisans.

"Dad?" Lexi slapped the top of his desk to get his attention. "Look at me."

Asher struggled to bring himself back to the present.

"Talk to me. You can't keep avoiding this."

He *would* talk to her. If she understood his past, maybe she would be less critical of the things he'd had to do to protect his family. If she understood his childhood, maybe she would stop asking about Harriet.

"I was born in Warsaw." His voice softened into velvet with the remembering. "When the Nazis began moving Jews into the ghetto, my family escaped, fleeing through the dark alleys and sewer tunnels late one night, carrying blankets and food. My parents, my brother and sister. I was twelve."

"Oh, Dad. You never told me this. Where'd you go?"

"To the *Kampinos* forest. My parents joined the partisans who were sabotaging supply routes. We children were sent to the family camp deep in the woods, where it was safer."

Of course, it was never safe in the forest. There were bands of Polish fascists searching for the partisans. Bandits, they called the Jews. And the Nazis searched too, since the partisans' actions destroyed their bridges and arsenals.

"One day, my sister and I went foraging for mushrooms and edible greens for the soup pot. We wandered along the banks of a swamp, where dead trees stood stark and bare in the water. She sang softly to me, a folk song in Yiddish."

The lyrics still eluded him, except in dreams.

"My sister was older, smart and responsible. The fighters thought their records would be safer in the family camp, so my sister carried the small leather journal which listed partisan actions in their sector deep in the pocket of her coat.

"That day in the woods we heard German voices. My sister made me hide in the hollow of a rotten log. I was small for my age. She covered me with branches and leaves. She tucked the leather book inside my shirt and told me to keep very quiet."

"You must have been so scared."

He wasn't sure what was true memory and what came from the dreams and the nightmares he'd had for decades. "I don't remember much. Bits of the songs she sang me. The putrid, dead smell of the swamp. She pushed my log into the tall reeds. And then she hid herself. But not well enough."

Lexi took his hand and squeezed it. Her cheeks were wet. Asher wondered if he had said enough. Enough so that she'd feel sorry for him and stop asking for more details. But, no. The story had its own motor. He had to finish.

"I heard her yell a warning in Yiddish. Then she screamed. I never saw my sister again. I spent the night floating in a rotten log on that dead pond. In the morning people from the camp found me. They never found her."

"What happened to the rest of your family?"

"All killed. In a year or two I was old enough to fight with the partisans. After the war my uncle in Brooklyn tried to get me a visa but by then the borders were closed to Jews." He glanced at Lexi, hoping sympathy would dissolve her anger, but she still frowned. "He bought me forged papers."

"What happened to the journal?"

"Years later I translated it into English. It was a list of partisan actions. Telegraph wires cut, railroad bridges blown up, grenades and rifles captured, turpentine confiscated, trains derailed." He swallowed hard. "I donated it to the Holocaust Museum in memory of Alexandra Elizabeth Blum."

"I'm named for her?"

He nodded, swiped his wet cheeks with his sleeve. "I'm sorry, Alexandra. So sorry."

"Sorry about what?"

"Everything."

"Why didn't you ever share this with me? Mom must've known, right?"

He shook his head. "Only a little. Living through something like that takes away your tongue. It silences you."

"I'm sorry about what happened, and I'm glad you finally told me.

But it's not enough. I need to know what's going on *now*. The whole story. What's going on with Mom? What happened to her?"

He covered his face with his hands. How could he tell her about Harriet, about the things he did? His actions had all seemed reasonable at the time, more than reasonable, really. They seemed right. Right and necessary and justified. Now those actions had somehow twisted themselves into something wrong. Evil, even. How could he unpeel the layers of what he did, of actions spanning decades?

He stared out his study window. The late afternoon clouds were dark and threatening. Then he turned to face his daughter. It was clear he had to tell her other things. But maybe not everything. Hopefully he could hang on to a little bit of self-respect.

ERIC GOLDEN

After the detectives left, Eric couldn't sit still. He should start cooking dinner, but food felt unimportant with a neighbor's life at stake. He kept thinking about his interview with the detectives. Why didn't he relay Asher's comment that he had messed up? He didn't really think Asher did anything to Iris, did he?

He walked upstairs and stood in the cramped hallway between the kids' bedrooms, listening to the normal sounds of their after-school life. Marc's computer spewed bedlam, and Morgan sang into the microphone plugged into her tablet. He thought about talking with Morgan about sneaking visits to Aggie, but what would he say? Bea would be furious, but he kind of liked the idea of Morgan sneaking out and making her own friends, even if the folks in Number Six were a bit odd.

If he was being honest with himself, part of what he liked was Morgan defying her mother. Things with Bea were pretty bad. Sometimes, thinking about Asher and Iris and their long marriage, he suspected that he and Bea would never make it. Even though he got that things weren't perfect next door, he wished for some of what the Blums had.

He should go try to talk to Asher, even though the last attempt had been unsuccessful. The old guy seemed to want to unload something onto his shoulders. But Eric didn't want to leave the kids alone. And he really wasn't sure he wanted to hear the details of whatever Asher meant when he said he messed up.

No, on this issue he was going to listen to Bea and keep his distance from Asher. Not entirely, of course. As soon as the detectives gave the green light, he'd organize a search party. It was practically part of his job as Azalea Court caretaker. He knew the cottages better than anyone else, and Iris wasn't likely to have traveled very far from home. For now, he'd start some homemade mac and cheese for dinner.

Comfort food was just what they all needed on a gloomy day that was about to erupt into a dark rain. On a sad day, when one of their small group of neighbors could be in big trouble.

IRIS BLUM

Iris watched how quickly Gloria removed the fabric and cardboard from the car windows, explaining she couldn't risk being stopped for driving with an obstructed view. She insisted that Iris hide, nestled in the rumpled bedding in the back of the station wagon. Cocooned by old quilts and comforters, Iris felt safe for the first time in weeks. A mix of pine and sweat scented the pillow, but it wasn't unpleasant. It was part of the homey feeling.

The best thing, aside from being away from Asher and his cruel secrets, was the cat curled against her chest and vibrating. Was that still considered purring, that deep silent shuddering? She had long wanted a cat, but Asher said animals brought dirt and disease into a home. If she and Asher survived this, he was going to have to change his mind about that. For starters.

That was the thing she didn't know. Did she want her marriage to survive? She'd been stewing for a month about what she'd learned about Asher's actions. But she hadn't thought things out well, hadn't planned, and she wasn't proud of herself for that. When she left early that morning, she just couldn't stay another second in that house with him.

"Penny for your thoughts?" Gloria called from the front seat.

"I'm afraid they're too confused to be worth even a penny, dear," Iris said. "Thank you so much for rescuing me."

"Do you want to tell me what's going on? Why you ran away?"

Gloria's voice floated over Iris's makeshift bed, her words hovering near the ceiling. It might be easy to have a conversation this way, not having to look at Gloria, to see her response to Iris's awkward story reflected in her eyes. Maybe not easy enough.

Iris considered avoiding the truth. In sixty-plus years with Asher, she had become pretty good at that. She could tell this kind woman, who probably did not need to get involved in her domestic problems, that she had exaggerated when she said running away. Maybe she could tell her a little bitty piece of the truth. She could say that she had always liked walking these trails, even though she now needed a cane for balance. She loved walking through the Community Gardens, especially after she learned that they once served as the kitchen garden for the state hospital. She loved walking along the Mill River, watching the seasonal transformations from water to ice and back again.

That was certainly *part* of the truth of her walk this morning. She had been out of breath by the time she reached the stone bench at the edge of the burial ground. The bench was cold on her butt. Asher would have corrected her word choice. *Derrière*, he would have said. Sometimes his English sounded impossibly stilted, reflecting that it wasn't his first language, even though he had scoured his mouth of any trace of a Yiddish accent. She had leaned forward on her cane, looking out at the burial ground. The November frost had melted in the midday sun and the Canada geese were making a racket in the next field over, thick with winter-cut corn stalks.

She had stopped at the bench to catch her breath and enjoy the view. To reread the plaque honoring those state hospital patients, known and unknown, buried in the field. She repeated that phrase out loud: *known and unknown.* Ironic how it mirrored her husband's profession. Asher liked to pretend they knew how to treat mental illness, but she listened between the lines and had long understood how deeply the experts were floundering, no matter what he wrote in that book of his.

Now she was the one floundering, since the afternoon a few weeks ago when she discovered Asher's papers about Harriet. But how much of this could she share with this kind woman, who had problems of her own?

"I don't know what to tell you," she said into the air. And she realized that the warmth, the gentle movement of the car, and how much stress she had been feeling, were making her very, very tired. "I'm so sleepy, dear. Would you mind if I took a little nap back here and told you all about it later?"

Iris closed her eyes and drifted. She didn't hear Gloria's response.

EVELYN TURNER

She had been watching for them, and she answered the detectives' knock right away. Curiosity, mostly, but she wanted to help find Iris if she could. If Iris wanted to be found. Or maybe she wanted to help Iris hide, if she had run away from her awful husband. Of course, Evelyn wasn't ready to talk about that with the cops. They might blame Iris instead of the real culprit in Number Two.

The detectives were polite, even when they questioned her repeatedly about why she made the 911 call. They implied, gently but with conviction, that she had some kind of beef with Dr. Blum. What had other people had been telling them? Maybe she *did* have a problem with Dr. Blum, but there were strong reasons for it. Once they let up on those questions Evelyn said she had another theory, that Dr. Blum's overbearing approach to Iris for decades had caused an episode of transient global amnesia. The cops exchanged sidelong glances when she said that.

"It's real," Evelyn insisted. "Google it. People lose all memory of the past and it can be triggered by stress. The memories come back though, eventually."

Looking at their faces, she let it drop. Clearly the officers weren't interested in her professional opinion. So, maybe her business had a couple of bad years, but she wasn't the only resident of Azalea Court with troubles. Rumor had it that the two women in Number Four had something unpleasant in their past. It was hard to believe that the Simon women were really in the Witness Protection Program like people gossiped, but stranger things had happened. And it was her duty to let the detectives know about all possibilities, wasn't it? Maybe somehow

Iris found out about the Witness Protection thing and the Number Four women had to shut her up. Okay, so that was a pretty unlikely scenario, but it was the cops' job to check it out, right?

Sometimes she felt unwelcome on the Court. A few neighbors had been unkind this past year as her home care agency circled the drain. The loss of her dream was a blow. It wasn't totally lost, really, just dwindled into dormancy. Maybe it was her own fault. She wasn't much of a businesswoman. Donnie said it was great that she wanted to provide personalized care with continuity and high-quality nursing, but it wasn't practical. It was impossible to find the right staff and to pay them enough, with insurance reimbursements coming so many months after the service was given.

She answered their questions until the detectives finally seemed satisfied that she had no ulterior motive, just had Iris's well-being at heart. They thanked her for the leaflets and even asked for some extra copies. The woman—McPhee—held Evelyn's eyes for a long moment right before they left.

"Remember," McPhee said. "Finding Mrs. Blum is our job. Sometimes that job can be dangerous. Any information you receive, or anything you think of that might help find her, must be communicated to us right away."

"Of course," Evelyn said, wondering what the detective thought she would do with that information, if not share it with the detectives. Wondering if her vague thoughts of helping Iris stay hidden were somehow visible to the cop. She was still shaking her head about that when the detectives left. She stood in the doorway and watched them walk to Number Four, then she wandered into the kitchen to refill her coffee cup.

The newspaper photo stared at her from the fridge, its red outline a bullseye on her fears. The brick facade of Old Main looked so solid, but it couldn't protect anyone, inside or out. The ancient copper beeches in front of the building leered at her across the decades, a tree chorus singing, *We saw what happened.* Actually, the massive tree trunks had shielded what happened. Blocked any possible rescue.

It had been spring of 1985. She was twenty-five years old, a nursing student. She wasn't enthusiastic about psychiatric nursing, but it was her last clinical rotation, her last weeks of being a student. She was anxious on her first day at the state hospital—it was imposing, even frightening—and she already knew she wanted to specialize in community health, so this was just something to get through. How bad could it be? Her neighbor Dr. Blum was the head shrink over there and the rotation was only six weeks. She'd been living with Donnie for almost a year and could walk there. Perfect, right?

Two weeks into the rotation, a medical student asked her to help him with a procedure on a patient. She was delighted with the assignment, relieved to avoid the stench of the locked ward, a witch's brew of mildew and urine and bleach. The med student was about her age, and she listened intently as he explained the procedure on their walk to the treatment room in another building. It was a sunny day, warm enough to leave her jacket behind as they walked across the grass past a huge copper beech tree to a small brick building. She had wondered where the patient was.

She should have suspected, should have known, there was no patient. By the time they were inside and she understood what was happening, the med student had locked the door of the old Coach House, had his hand over her mouth, and a knee pushing under her clean white student nurse uniform. All these years later, she never forgot the horsey smell of the dirt floor. His blue eyes. Garlic on his breath and then garlic spit on her arm, where he bit her, branded her, when he was finished.

Donnie tried to be supportive when it happened, and he didn't get angry that she wouldn't let him touch her for months. But he thought she should be over it by now. Why should one unwanted sexual encounter be so huge, he kept asking. She had never been able to explain it to him. Her rapist didn't hurt her that much physically and thankfully hadn't given her any disease or pregnancy. The bite on her arm got infected, but it healed with antibiotics. She rubbed the scar absently.

It wasn't a matter of shame, not really. She knew it wasn't her fault. She hadn't invited or provoked his attack in any way. She reported it to her instructor and the hospital administration but refused to file a police report, despite the clamor of friends insisting she do so. That afternoon reinforced her decision to avoid medical institutions of any kind. To take care of people in the haven of their homes, although she had since learned that some homes weren't much of a refuge.

She shook herself out of her memories. The hospital memorial dedication was in two days. Even though she knew that reliving old pain wasn't healthy, she couldn't stop her brain from going back. She needed to get out of the house and do something useful. She would look for Iris on her own. She knew Iris, and Iris trusted her. If anyone could find the woman, *she* would be that person.

GANDALF SIMON

Jess went into the kitchen to brew tea. Gandalf wondered why people always made tea when big feelings were involved. A learned cultural response, she supposed, since she was unaware of evidence that chemical compounds in tea leaves soothe emotional pain. She straightened the piles of newspaper on the end table and sat on the sofa, waiting for the four-minute steep time Jess believed critical for good tea. She thought about Maine islands and the cold room and being interrogated. She remembered escaping and the cave and the hurricane and the terror. All the tea in the world couldn't ease those memories.

The doorbell rang and Jess, who was facing the window, stood up.

"It's the police," Jess said. "Do you want to hang out in your study, and I'll deal with them?"

Gandalf nodded and hurried into the back room, hoping that Jess wouldn't forget her tea, still two minutes shy of perfect. She left the door open enough to hear the conversation in the living room but closed it after hearing the same questions the detectives had asked her earlier.

She knew she should stop dwelling on the irrelevant fact that Iris grew up on Storm Harbor, a short boat ride across the Sound from Hurricane Island, but the coincidence felt momentous. The old Gandalf, the person she had been before being kidnapped and interrogated by Homeland Security, would argue with that last thought. She would dismiss it as simple coincidence, of no importance. But the new Gandalf was not so certain. The new Gandalf balanced her emotions on a knife's edge. Some days all it took was a heavy rain to send her spiraling back to Hurricane Island and terror. She closed the heavy curtains in her study.

Ten minutes later, Jess opened the study door. "They're gone," she said. "Your tea is ready."

The tea was hot, with a splash of milk and a teaspoon of honey, just the way she liked it. She sipped it and set it down on the newspapers on the end table, centering the cup over the face of a politician she only vaguely recognized.

"How did it go with the detectives?" Gandalf asked.

Jess grinned. "Fine, except that they asked whether either of us had ever been part of the Witness Protection Program."

Gandalf laughed. "I have never understood how that rumor got started, or how it followed us up here from Manhattan. But it's always good for a laugh."

"I'll take any humor that's offered today." She took Gandalf's hand. "Are you okay? What happened to upset you?"

"Thank you," Gandalf said. "For coming home early."

"Your message sounded pretty distraught."

"I didn't mean to frighten you."

Jess shook her head. "Explain it to me. What's the connection to Hurricane Island?"

Safe in her home, with hot tea and her beloved, none of it seemed as frightening. "It is just that Iris, the missing woman, was born on Storm Harbor. Seeing those two words on the policewoman's flyer triggered something, and I was back there on Hurricane Island, shivering and terrified."

Jess took her hand. "Sounds as if it could have been a PTSD flashback, like we talked about. I've been reading about the good results people are getting with Eye Movement Desensitization and Reprocessing. Remember, I mentioned a couple of therapists in town specialize in EMDR?"

Gandalf stood up abruptly, knocking into the table and sloshing tea on the politician's perfect hair. "I told you I don't want any therapy, no matter what the initials are. No one has permission to muck around in my head. No one. Okay?"

Jess patted the sofa. "It's all okay. Come cuddle with me and drink your tea. It'll calm your nerves."

It was not okay, but it would have to do.

TIMOTHY BEAUJOLAIS

The rude, hooded woman ran out of their house, and Imani started crying. It was so amazing how their baby picked up the emotions adults thought they were hiding. Timothy couldn't calm her down. Winda's response was to return to the kitchen and furiously arrange utensils in the silverware drawer. Timothy grabbed his jacket and zipped it up over the Bjorn, then kissed Winda's cheek.

"I'm taking Imani for a walk. Maybe she'll fall asleep in the fresh air."

Winda adjusted the hood of the baby's sweater, kissed her forehead, and nodded.

The green area in the center of the circle was empty. No one was in sight except for two police detectives in front of Number Two. Timothy sang softly to Imani as he walked towards the cops. He was self-conscious about his walk, the half-sway, half-jiggle movement he had watched Winda use since Imani was a newborn and had been trying to mimic ever since. It was fluid and lovely when Winda did it; on him it was cumbersome at best, ludicrous for sure. But it worked, and Imani's eyes were already at half-mast by the time he reached the detectives.

"I'm Timothy Beaujolais," he said. "My wife and daughter and I just moved in today." He pointed to their house. The female cop introduced herself and said she'd seen the moving van.

"How's the search going?" Timothy asked.

"Nothing substantial yet."

"I'd like to take my baby for a walk," he told her. "It's the best way to get this peanut to nap. Is it okay to walk along the river? Is it safe?"

She handed him a leaflet with a phone number hand-written on the bottom. "Just keep your eyes open and please call me if you see anything suspicious. The canine team and drone search are just finishing up." She pointed up at the heavy clouds. "Might want to make it a short walk. It's going to rain."

"Better get going then." He turned away, then turned back. "Which way is the river?"

McPhee pointed west to the trees, dark now against the dusk.

The path was clearly well used, wide and cleared of branches and rocks. To the left, the Community Garden sign welcomed visitors. Would he and Winda have time to grow vegetables in this new life? Up ahead, the path turned downhill into thicker forest. He looked up at the sky and down into the trees and decided Imani's nap was more important than staying dry.

The path was rockier here, and he needed to watch his step, not an easy thing with the mound of his daughter blocking his view of his feet. But the soft whistle of her sleeping breaths was worth the careful footing, and soon the path turned alongside a small river. He found himself singing *thula sana*, for his own soothing rather than Imani's this time. The trail followed the river past last year's stubby cornstalks that were home to extended families of geese, then turned uphill again at a large open field. Out in the open, he felt raindrops on his head, and darkness was falling quickly.

He pulled the baby carrier headpiece over Imani and put up his hood as well. Large raindrops spattered on his jacket and on the ground. Looking around, he wondered what the fastest way home might be— back the way he came, or up ahead? In front of him, on a bench at the crest of the hill, a person sat motionless. For a moment, he wondered if it could be the missing old woman, but the posture was that of a younger person. In any case, he or she might know the quickest route home and he hurried uphill to ask.

The person on the bench was opening an umbrella as he reached her. He was curious about the plaque and stone monument near the bench, but reading them would have to wait for better weather.

"Hey," he called out. "Can you tell me the quickest way back to Azalea Court?"

"That's where I'm going. Come share my umbrella." She held it over Imani, who was still sleeping, oblivious to the raindrops on her cheek. They walked briskly uphill, away from the river.

"I'm Evelyn," she said. "Number Three on the Court."

"I'm Timothy. My wife and daughter and I just moved into Number Five." He laughed. "Like, three hours ago!"

"Welcome," she said. "Now let's hoof it before the skies really open up."

"Any news about the woman who's missing?" he asked as they walked.

Evelyn shook her head. "No. I've been looking for her. And now this rain."

FRIDAY EVENING

What We Thought We Knew:
Tonics, including some stimulants, are the principal medicines, assisted, as the case may require, by nervines, soporifics, alternatives or cathartics. The lancet is emphatically an instrument of the past, and cups and leeches are very nearly in the same category.

—Dr. Pliny Earle,
Northampton State Hospital Annual Report, 1868

THE WOMEN

As dark fell, we hunkered down in our cottages, feeling both safe and in danger, both warm at home and shivering in the sad chill of the evening. Those of us who knew Iris worried deeply about her. She wasn't that frail, but recent weeks had aged her, or our idea of her anyway. Those of us who knew her only to wave "Good Morning" across the street thought about her too, but we mused more about our own safety, about how fragile our constructed lives could turn out to be.

We wouldn't have admitted it or even talked about it with our closest family or friends, but most of us were wondering whether the tales were true. You know. You've heard them. All those stories of our neighborhood being haunted by restless souls, by the ghosts of folks who didn't belong incarcerated in a mental hospital, or those who did belong, but never received the treatment that might help them. There have been books and films, websites and musical events, poems, and songs—all trying to understand what happened on these few acres of hilltop beauty over a century and a half of well-meaning bumbling.

In the fading light that evening, as we washed up after a hot meal, watched the news on television, and cuddled with our loved ones, we tried not to picture our Iris alone and cold and maybe hurt—or worse. We couldn't help wondering if we had tempted fate by living here, among the unsettled thrown-away lives.

Had those ghosts somehow taken Iris?

ARNIE NORTH

It was worrisome, all this attention on Azalea Court. Not that he'd done anything wrong, but he still worried. Aggie and he had never fit in and they never would. One thing they had learned was that not fitting in usually meant trouble.

When the doorbell rang, he ignored it.

GLORIA

Maybe it was the dark or the drumming rain, exhaustion or stress or simply advanced age. Or perhaps the soporific delight of a cat sleeping against her chest combined with the motion of the car. Whatever the reason, the old woman had slipped into a deep sleep in the back of Gloria's station wagon. Her mouth hung half-open in that terribly vulnerable way that always reminded Gloria of her father in his last days.

She didn't know where it was safe to go. Safe for her and for Iris. She didn't like feeling responsible for the woman, especially with the cops looking for her. Most days Gloria felt she could barely take care of herself. But she had to admit to a small bit of gratitude that she wasn't alone. Even this meager portion of human company was welcome. Even company that had danger attached. Even for just a few hours. Iris showing up made Gloria aware of how deeply lonely she was. Despite the added danger, Gloria liked feeling like she was taking care of someone again, someone who needed her.

But those feelings didn't point her in a direction or a destination. Gas wasn't cheap, and she couldn't drive forever. With the old woman in the car, she didn't feel comfortable going to either of the makeshift campsites in town where the homeless congregated. Someone might recognize Iris—her photo would be on television and the internet soon if it weren't already—and turn her in for the reward, or because a cop might be more forgiving the next time a panhandling regulation or town ordinance was breached.

"How long did I sleep?" Iris asked from the back of the wagon.

"Maybe an hour. How do you feel?"

"Better. Where are we?"

"Just driving around," Gloria said. "We couldn't stay there. Too many cops out searching for you. Now that it's dark, they'll search harder."

"I'm sorry," Iris said. "I've put you at risk, dear. I just don't know what else to do."

"Is there any place you can go, any family or friends?"

"No." Iris was silent for a moment. "I'm hungry. Can we get some food? I can pay for it."

Twenty minutes later they were parked in the McDonald's lot devouring burgers and fries, licking salt off their fingers and slurping thick milkshakes.

"Would you believe I've never eaten at McDonald's before?" Iris said. "This stuff is good!"

Gloria laughed. "I'm honored to be the one to introduce you to delicious junk food. But seriously, where can I take you? Do you have family, other than your husband?"

"My daughter Lexi," Iris said. "I know that she would help me, but right now she'll be with her father and the police, helping in the search. I don't know how to contact her without them knowing."

Gloria poured a small amount of milkshake into Canary's bowl. The cat sniffed it and stepped away. Gloria laughed and scratched under the cat's chin. "Too sweet for you?"

"Oh." Gloria looked at Iris. "What about your cell phone? Is it with you?"

Iris grinned. "I left it at home. I've watched those cop shows on TV. That's how they locate people, by pinging their phones. I figured I could find a phone booth if I needed one. Which I don't think I will."

"I have a friend in cohousing who lets me use her shower and guest room for a night now and then. We could go there and figure out what's next in the morning."

Iris sniffled. "Thank you, dear. You've saved my life."

"You're not safe yet," Gloria said.

Iris didn't answer. Gloria felt bad and talked to fill up the silence.

"Someone once told me that the best place to hide is in plain sight, where no one would think to look for you because it's so obvious. In your case, that might be back on Azalea Court. Is there someone there, a neighbor who you trust to let you stay with them?"

"Not really," Iris said. "Eric is a sweet young man, but I'm sure he feels closer to my husband than to me. And his wife, well, I don't think Bea would go out of her way for anyone. Probably the best bet would be Evelyn. She's a nurse, and she cares about me. But asking her for help feels too risky. I'm afraid she's not so good at keeping secrets."

Gloria moved the wrappers from her lap so the cat could curl up. "I guess as a last resort we could get into the basement of the Haskell Building on the old state hospital grounds. There are state offices there now, but they rarely use the basement. It's full of old furniture and stuff. Maybe we could make you a hiding place down there."

Iris didn't answer. Gloria saw tears snaking down her cheeks.

"What is it?"

"Nothing, dear. It's just that it would be ironic for me to hide in a state hospital building. That place and its ghosts are the reason I'm in this awful mess."

DETECTIVE McPHEE

There's something so forlorn about a cold and windblown November rain. McPhee shivered in her car, watching waves of water slap against the windshield. She checked her watch. Just after six and already totally dark. It would be good to spend the evening at home, if she ever got there, although nothing would keep her brain from puzzling over Azalea Court and Iris Blum. There was nothing else for her to do here tonight, except worry. She might as well head back to the station, write up her report, and talk to the night shift detectives. Make sure a patrol car drove around Azalea Court and the surrounding streets every couple of hours. Just in case.

She looked down at her notebook and checked the residents off her list: Eric Golden and his kids, Jess Simon, Evelyn Turner, and the new guy in Number Five. The neighbors didn't seem to have any relevant information, but she had to go through the motions. And besides, you never knew what little tidbit might come out if you kept asking the right questions. Something that could make all the difference. Not something that was pure fantasy, like the Witness Protection Program rumor. She'd check it out, of course. But, really, how silly.

The canine team handler called and reported that the dog picked up Mrs. Blum's scent along the river and at the burial ground bench but lost it again on the road near the dog park. Nothing after that. She texted the drone operator, but he didn't see anything either. He promised to send McPhee the video file, so she could look for herself.

In the morning she'd return to Number Six. She didn't think there was anything to it, but she had to follow-up on the report of a stranger wearing a hoodie seen at the burial grounds, in the vicinity of a woman who fit Mrs. Blum's description. Elder Services had promised to come by first thing in the morning. And at some point, she'd have to bring Dr. Blum to the station for a formal interview, videotaped and following all the rules and regs. In the morning, she'd gather together the neighbors who wanted to help search. No reason they couldn't begin that tomorrow, if the weather cooperated.

But this evening, she would try to relax. Her wife had the night off too. Maybe they would order take-out sushi and build a blaze in the fireplace. But even with a glass of wine, she knew she wouldn't sleep well. She never did during a big case. Especially one like this, where all the personalities and histories and secrets swirled in her head. No, she would be awake most of the night worrying about what could have happened to Mrs. Iris Blum.

WINDA BEAUJOLAIS

Winda couldn't sleep.

She slipped quietly from bed, careful not to wake Timothy, and stood over Imani's crib watching her make sucking motions with pursed lips. What did her daughter dream about without words to frame the pictures? Listening to the rain, she maneuvered around the cardboard packing boxes piled along the walls and looked out every window. She couldn't help worrying about the missing old woman out there, cold and alone.

In the dark of the unfamiliar house, she let herself consider the possibility that she and Timothy had made a major mistake. What were they thinking, leaving their crowded, noisy, variegated Brooklyn neighborhood for this place? The teaching job had felt like such a plum, so convenient and perfect, but danger could be lurking. Maybe her dark skin was simply a box to be checked off in the college's diversity portfolio. Maybe the odd, hooded woman from next door wasn't the only one who would look at her beloved daughter and back away.

Or it could be just bad luck that they moved in on the day an old woman with dementia wandered off. The police would probably find Mrs. Blum in the morning—or maybe she was already tucked into bed with her husband—and everything would return to normal on Azalea Court. Yes, that was most likely what would happen.

Still, she heard her grandmother's voice in her head. *Would it hurt to pray to your ancestors to bless your new home?* Winda didn't actively pray to the elders in her family who had passed on, not like her mother and aunties did, but she didn't entirely dismiss the practice either. Timothy had never questioned the small shrine she kept by her bed so why should she feel slightly embarrassed by it? Especially here, in this place so foreign to her upbringing, it could be a comfort.

She smiled to herself as her grandmother's voice continued. *Listen to your Bibi. The rain is a good sign, but it may not be enough. Let us guide you. We are with you.*

SATURDAY MORNING

What We Thought We Knew:
It appears to the present writer that there is about as close an analogy between pneumonia and insanity as there is between a broken bone and a broken promise.

—Dr. Pliny Earle,
Northampton State Hospital Superintendent, 1880

LEXI BLUM

The thing she had never told her father was that in her own way she was as obsessed with the state hospital as he was. She had downloaded the State Library's annual hospital reports onto her laptop and read them carefully, studying the causes of death, the reasons for hospitalization, the treatments that read more like medieval torture than therapies. She was most curious about the women incarcerated there. *Here.* She thought of them as the lost women. The ones whose husbands tired of them, who didn't fit the norms of their time. Women like her, who didn't want to be wives and mothers. She thought of her interest as the flip side of her father's research for his book. Maybe one day she'd write her own book to bring those lost women back to life. She wanted to be like that performance artist who blasted Bach from the ruins—before they were demolished—to honor the missing voices.

The hospital was on her mind when she opened her eyes Saturday morning in her childhood bedroom. Her mother had turned it into a sewing room, but Lexi's old twin bed was still there and a few discarded clothes remained in the bottom drawer of the dresser, pushed to the back by skeins of yarn her mother would probably never use. Her first waking thought was about one of the state hospital stories she'd been collecting, a true story about a patient who didn't belong there—*here*—but was committed by a husband who had grown tired of her.

She had always been fascinated by the state hospital. When she was a kid and had a day off school, she begged her father to take her to work with him, but he never would. So, she snuck around, peering into windows. She found the doors that staff propped open with a bit of wood when they went outside for a smoke. She and Donnie sometimes wandered in the basement, through warrens of musty corridors stacked with unused stuff. Braver kids partied in the old tunnels, but their dank mustiness and moldy shadows creeped Lexi out too much.

She had slept later than usual and woke up feeling groggy and disoriented. She had tried talking with her father last night, but he was clearly exhausted and spent. He was ninety-four, after all. After he went to bed, promising to tell her everything in the morning, she drove home to pick up a few things, figuring she'd stay with him for at least the weekend. Back on Azalea Court, she couldn't fall asleep. The mattress was too soft, and her mind was racing. It must have been after three in the morning that she finally conked out.

Maybe a shower would clear her head. The house was quiet when she opened the door and she slipped into the bathroom. When she walked into the hallway twenty minutes later, towel around her dripping hair, there were voices in the living room. Lexi did not recognize the voice of the woman who was speaking in soft sentences, but her father's voice was clear, as was the harsh tone he used with her as a child when she said something he considered stupid.

"Are you accusing me of something?" he asked. "Are you saying I can't keep my own wife safe? Do you know who I am?"

Lexi moved closer to the living room, still hidden from the voices. That edge in her father's voice had always driven her crazy. She considered joining the conversation to maybe learn something, even in her robe and towel, but eavesdropping was safer.

"No one is accusing you of anything," the soft voice said. "We're just concerned about finding your wife."

"I don't need your help," her father insisted. "Get out of my house."

At the sound of footsteps and the front door opening and closing, Lexi slipped back into the bedroom, heart pounding. How could he act that way?

She dressed quickly and found her father sitting at the kitchen table.

"Who was that?" Lexi asked. "Who was just here?"

"Elder Services. A total waste of taxpayer money." He opened the newspaper. "Will you make coffee?"

She talked her way through the process so he could learn, just in case. But he wasn't listening.

While the coffee was dripping, she made toast and opened a jar of jam that she brought back from the Cape a couple of years before. As her father took his first bite, she sat across from him at the table.

"Time to talk, Dad."

He shook his head, but she held up her hand. "You promised."

"After breakfast."

While she washed the dishes, her father slipped away to his study. She followed him there, dragging in a chair from the kitchen.

"Time to talk," Lexi said. "Tell me why Mom left. It has something to do with Harriet, doesn't it?"

"It's complicated," he said.

She waited. After a long pause, he continued.

"Harriet was your mother's best friend, but she wasn't good for Iris. She threatened everything we wanted to make of our lives." He squeezed his eyes shut. "I'm as good a citizen as the next man, but I know how things work. My family comes first. That's what I thought then, when it happened, and that's what I think now."

"When *what* happened? Tell me about Harriet."

"They grew up together on that damn island. I met them at Brooklyn College. They were undergrads and I was in med school. At first, we all had a good time together. Classes and politics. Half of Brooklyn College was in the Party."

"The Party?"

"The Communist Party. It was very popular on campuses in those days, actively protesting economic inequality. It was all okay, until one day it wasn't." He paused. "I lived through the war in Europe. I had seen very bad things, and I could see what was coming here."

"You told me that. But what does it have to do with Harriet?"

"It was getting dangerous. Harriet was deeply involved in Party organizing. So, I told Iris she couldn't see Harriet anymore."

"You told her she couldn't see her best friend?" This seemed extreme, even for her father.

"It was *dangerous*. You don't know what it was like in those years. People were terrified. People were ruined."

"Still," she said. "Her best friend. Was Mom in the Communist Party too?"

"No. But people were considered guilty if they associated with Communists. It was a terrible time. I had to forbid Iris to see Harriet, for her own good."

Her disbelief and disgust must have shown on her face.

"You don't know what it was like," he said. "The Rosenbergs were on Death Row. All Jews were suspect, and it was extremely hard for us to find jobs. Your Mom and I were about to be married." He hesitated. "Harriet was a danger to us."

"Did she do it, stop seeing her best friend?"

"I thought so."

"What do you mean? What happened?"

Her father stood up, and she could see that his shakiness was real. "Enough for now. I'm too tired to talk more."

"No. You can't stop now. Finish the story. What happened? What did you do?

He sat down, collapsing into the chair. "Okay. Okay. What I did was to write an anonymous letter to the high school where Harriet taught chemistry, telling them that she was a member of the Communist Party. That was enough to get her fired." He rubbed his face. "Harriet was called before HUAC."

"HUAC?"

"The House Unamerican Activities Committee. Harriet refused to cooperate and spent six months in prison for contempt."

Her *father* did those things? "Mom must have been furious."

"She almost called off the wedding. But it was Harriet or us. I had to protect my family. My wife, my job, you."

"I wasn't born yet. Don't blame this on me."

"You were coming. I did it for you too."

Lexi just stared at him.

"I know you're judging me, Alexandra. But you must remember this. Jews are never ever safe. Here or in Europe or anywhere. They can come for us at any time. As Jews, Harriet and Iris should have known these things. *You* should know these things. But Iris didn't understand, and neither did Harriet."

ERIC GOLDEN

Bea left with the kids for Saturday morning soccer practice just as the detective's car drove onto Azalea Court. Eric grabbed his jacket and met Detective McPhee as she pulled on her gloves.

"Any news?" he asked.

She shook her head.

"Can we organize a search party this morning?" he asked. "If the dogs are done, and the drone is finished? Most people are home today, and we know our neighborhood better than you folks do. We might find something your searchers missed."

"Sure," the detective said. "Just tell people that if they find something, anything at all, they should call me. Not investigate it themselves. They might compromise evidence." She looked at Eric intently. "It's possible that there could be some danger. People should stay in groups and be careful."

By midmorning, Eric had gathered his neighbors on the Circle benches. The rain was over, but thick clouds and gusts of wind sent Evelyn home for a heavier coat. She and Donnie were ready to search, and the two women from Number Four joined them. Aggie and Arnold were working the weekend, but the new guy in Number Five showed up, his baby wide-eyed and smiling in the front pack strapped to his chest.

"I'm Timothy," he said, shaking hands with everyone. "I don't know the neighborhood yet, of course, but I'd like to help."

Evelyn handed him a flyer. "That's Iris. The woman who's missing."

"We should check all the backyards," Eric said. "Plus, the gardens and the route Iris liked to take along the river and past the burial grounds. Who wants to do what?"

Before anyone could answer, Lexi came stomping out of her parents' house and onto the Circle. "I can't stay in that house another second," she announced. "Can I search with you guys? I need to do something useful."

Donnie put his arm around her shoulders and squeezed. "I'm so sorry, Lexi. This must be so hard."

She nodded. "Thanks. Where should I look, Eric?"

"Either the gardens, backyards, or your Mom's favorite walk by the river."

"I'll take the gardens," Lexi said.

"Gandalf and I will come with you," Jess offered.

Donnie and Eric decided to check out the backyards. Evelyn looked at Timothy and said, "Come on. I'll show you the different trails to the burial ground, where we met in the rain yesterday. Iris loved that walk, although it was getting harder for her to manage."

Donnie and Eric set out in silence, moving from one yard to the next. They peered under screen porches, inside gazebos and storage sheds filled with shovels and cross-country skis and cobwebs. Wind-blown leaves covered bags of unused mulch and discarded toasters. Nothing was locked—that wasn't how people lived on Azalea Court—so the search went quickly. They started together in the front of each cottage, separated to check the side yards, and met up in the back.

"Anything?" Donnie asked as they finished Number Four.

"Nada. But why would Iris leave her house and hide in a backyard?"

"If she has Alzheimer's?"

"I guess," Eric said. "Asher says her dementia is a kind that progresses very quickly."

Donnie shrugged. "Evelyn says it doesn't seem like Alzheimer's. And she doesn't trust Dr. Blum."

"Asher's not a bad guy." Eric believed that, really wanted to believe it, even though he wished he was more certain that the old man was being completely honest.

Donnie shrugged. "Maybe not. But Evelyn has a thing about the guy, thinks he's evil. And she's totally freaked out about the Memorial thing tomorrow. I wonder if he'll still speak at it, with his wife missing and everything."

"Who knows," Eric said. "Who the fuck knows what's going on with Asher Blum."

IRIS BLUM

She woke up in a strange bed, a strange room, deep in shadows. A thin frame of light around a small window near the ceiling suggested a basement bedroom. The sounds of a shower seeped under a closed door. Her watch said eleven. She hadn't slept past seven-thirty in decades. She closed her eyes, trying to remember the dream floating just out of reach. Harriet was there, looking like she had in college, and she was trying to tell Iris something important, but her body kept fading. Iris drifted, thoughts shifting from the dream to the impossible lifetime ago that was yesterday. What had she been thinking, just leaving like that, with no plan other than to get away from Asher and the big mess he had made of everything?

She understood her part in the mess and accepted her small portion of responsibility. She knew how much Asher hated being lied to. She understood how frightened he had been as the government started demanding loyalty oaths, how he blamed Harriet for pulling them into dangerous territory. But Asher refused to understand how grateful Iris had been to have her best friend waiting for her at Brooklyn College when she arrived as a freshman. Harriet had secured a double room for them and could introduce Iris to a group of like-minded students.

Things don't turn out the way you expect, do they? All she wanted was to have both Asher and Harriet in her life, her sweetheart and her best friend. Harriet was her friend since forever. There weren't a lot of kids in the island school, so the two girls would have been in each other's lives even if they didn't hit it off. But they did. They did everything together, from two-wheelers to Tampax. No surprise Iris followed Harriet to Brooklyn, and they both took chemistry. Harriet was pre-med. In those days it wasn't easy to have a career and a family and Iris wasn't sure what she wanted until the moment she met Asher, filling in for a sick buddy teaching their chem lab.

After that lab the three of them spent time together—what little time Asher could spare. They studied hard and all had jobs, but there was so much else to think about. It was 1949 and they were all worried about Russia and the Cold War and Senator McCarthy's witch hunt. As time went on, Iris spent more time with Asher, and Harriet became more involved with politics. Asher worried when Harriet joined the Communist Party, and he asked Iris not to spend time with Harriet. That was impossible of course, but she didn't flaunt their friendship. She met Harriet at times and places Asher would never know about, so life was peaceful.

Peaceful on the surface, anyway. Asher occasionally made snide comments about Harriet, which Iris ignored. Harriet also expressed her dislike of Asher. "He's no good for you, Iris," Harriet warned. "I don't trust the man."

Then the letter came from the government. Iris would never forget that day. It was a month before their wedding and it was Monday, the only day Asher got off early. When Iris got home from classes, he was waiting in her apartment.

"This letter." He waved it in the air. "What's going on?"

"What is it?" Iris asked.

"The FBI claims you are a member of the Brooklyn Bookstore Association?"

Iris met his eyes. "I was," she said. "Freshman and sophomore years. Remember? If you joined, you got a discount on textbooks, and there was that women's book discussion group I liked to attend."

"That store was a subversive organization. It's on the list. I had to sign a loyalty oath, swearing that I wasn't a Communist. I could lose my new job before we even get to Massachusetts. How could you endanger us like that?"

"I joined for the discount." She grabbed the letter and waved it in his face. "It was just a bookstore. Look at the other organizations on that stupid Attorney General's list: the Chopin Cultural Center, the Committee for the Negro in the Arts, the Committee for the Protection of the Bill of Rights."

"It's not up to you to decide," he argued. "They decide who's subversive."

She stared at him. "You're never home. I'm lonely. I joined for the company."

That was decades ago, and she was still lonely. Iris stared at the bright frame of light around the window, trying to banish the past and bring herself back to this time, this room, wherever it was. Those early days with Harriet were gone and whatever redo she could imagine, whatever path she might have taken to lead to a different ending, well that was gone too. All she had left was her own sad self, living with the knowledge that she hadn't saved Harriet from Asher.

Maybe she could have prevented it all, if only she had stood up to him. If she had said she wouldn't stay with him, wouldn't marry him, if she couldn't have her best friend too. But she hadn't done that, hadn't even tried to gather her strength to try. Didn't that make her partly responsible for Harriet's death? She hadn't known what Asher did, imprisoning Harriet in his hospital, but she had felt that something was very wrong. And when she lost their baby, her pain was magnified by thoughts of missing Harriet, thoughts she had no words to explain.

She squeezed her eyes closed against the blurring, brimming memories, images of making friendship bracelets with Harriet or racing on their bikes to the most isolated island quarry, their favorite summer fun. "Slowpoke!" they yelled back and forth to each other.

"Iris? Iris! Are you okay?" Gloria was shaking her shoulder. She wore a terry bathrobe and a towel around her hair. Her skin looked scrubbed pink, almost raw.

"I'm fine, dear. Just half-dreaming. Remembering long-ago times." She looked around. "Where are we? I don't remember coming here."

"My friend's place in cohousing. You were so deeply asleep my friend's son had to practically carry you into the house." Gloria laughed. "I've never seen anyone sleep like that. You didn't even wake up for dinner."

"Wait," Iris said. "Did your friends see me? I'm sure my photograph is all over television and the newspapers."

"Just their teenage son, and all old people look alike to kids that age, if they even notice you at all. We're alone here now. Come upstairs and eat, and then we'll figure out what's next. You must be starving."

DONNIE TURNER

Eric and Donnie finished searching the backyard of Number Six.

"That's the last one," Eric said, pinching off a shriveled mum flower in a neglected side bed. "No sign of her."

"You going to the Garden Memorial program tomorrow?" Donnie asked.

"I guess. I feel bad for Asher having to give a speech, with Iris missing."

"I can't believe my wife wants to attend it, after everything that happened to her at the hospital."

The Circle was empty. Donnie wondered if any of the other searchers were having better luck. In any case, he didn't want to go back in his house, where that clipping on the fridge would stare at him. He turned to Eric. "I mean, why would Evelyn want to go to a ceremony commemorating the worst time of her life? That's masochistic, isn't it?"

Eric nodded but didn't say anything. Donnie wouldn't know how to respond to another guy saying that either. They stood by the benches in the Circle. Donnie kicked at the leaves piled at the bench legs.

"Guess I've got some more raking to do this weekend," Eric said, sitting down.

Donnie sat on the facing bench. He'd lived almost next door to Eric and Bea for years, but they'd never socialized beyond the casual conversation. Eric seemed like an okay guy, even if he was pretty tight with Dr. Blum. But Evelyn called Bea a stuck-up bitch. She would be furious if he told Eric anything, even though what happened to her wasn't her fault, none of it was her fault, but she acted like she was still ashamed.

"I wish I could convince Evelyn not to go to the ceremony," Donnie said. "Something bad happened to her at that place, and everyone hushed it up. Blum said it would negatively impact their relationships with the medical schools who used the place for clinical rotations. Maybe even affect their state funding." Donnie made a fist with one hand and slammed it into the palm of the other hand, over and over.

"No wonder you don't like Asher."

Donnie rubbed his hands hard across his face. "I have no use for Dr. Blum and neither does Evelyn. When it happened, I wanted to report it to the police, but Evelyn refused. She never really got over it. The strange thing is that she never used to talk about it, but since Iris went missing, she talks about nothing else."

"So how did she become friends with Iris?"

"At first, I think she just wanted to find out about Dr. Blum, gather dirt about him. Maybe get back at him somehow." Donnie shook his head. "My wife can be vindictive. But she really liked Iris, and they became friends." He shook his head again, hard, then stood up. "Life is funny, isn't it?"

"Let me know if I can do anything. Tomorrow."

Donnie turned back. "Oh, yeah. Tomorrow will be great fun in my family."

GANDALF SIMON

Was this a good idea, walking around the gardens with the missing woman's daughter? She and Jess barely knew Lexi. She did not live on the Court, but she visited her parents regularly; at least it seemed that way to Gandalf. She and Jess didn't have many friends and Gandalf knew that was her fault, so having another person to walk and talk with—even someone whose mother was missing and possibly worse—was a welcome change in a twisted kind of way. And Gandalf had always been curious about the Community Gardens.

"I walked through the gardens yesterday from where I parked," Lexi said. "I didn't see any sign of my mother. But we'll take a closer look."

"Do your parents have a garden plot?" Jess asked.

Lexi shook her head. "Mom loved to grow flowers in the yard, but she's arthritic and can't do much anymore."

They reached the gravel road circling the seven acres of garden, carved by footpaths into square plots. Surprisingly orderly and neat for something as messy as dirt and dead plants and compost. Lexi pointed to the left. "Let's start here and go up and down the rows, okay?"

Gandalf nodded and tightened the scarf around her throat, studying the garden squares on both sides of the path. At least the rain was over. Rainstorms, with wind and raw chill, sent her reeling back to the island, to the quarry, to an urge to escape she could only soften by curling up in bed and covering her head with pillows. She rarely came outside in daylight, but most nights she walked for an hour or longer on the sidewalks and pathways of the neighborhood, trying to tire herself out enough to sleep.

They walked in silence. Some plots were neat, with dead plant material removed and rake marks visible in the partly frozen soil. A few plots were covered with strips of burlap held down by stones and bricks. Others sprouted brown stalks, dead leaves and the occasional shriveled tomato or pepper.

"Mom!" Lexi called out. "Mom, are you here?"

"Not many places a person could find shelter here, are there?" Jess commented.

Lexi's face crumpled. "She gets cold so easily. She'll freeze out here if we don't find her."

Jess put her arm around Lexi and hugged her. For the hundredth time in their lives together, Gandalf wished she could be as spontaneously warm as Jess.

"What about that?" Jess pointed to an overgrown plot containing a wooden structure. It could have once been a grape arbor, or perhaps a greenhouse abandoned to the elements. Black plastic was draped across the top and sides and nailed down, but one loose piece flapped in the chilly wind. Lexi picked her way between tall stalks that might have grown Brussel sprouts. She lifted the blowing edge and peered inside.

"Anything?" Jess asked.

"Just tools and buckets." Lexi rejoined the women on the path bordered by piles of wood chips and deep moist dirt, dried brush and leaves. "I keep trying to understand, but I just don't know what Mom was thinking, leaving the house like that."

"Do you think it was her dementia?" Jess asked.

Lexi stopped walking and turned to face Jess. "I'm not convinced my mother has dementia. Her symptoms started too rapidly. I've been reading about Alzheimer's. This, whatever it is that my mother has, doesn't feel right."

"What are you saying? What do you think happened to your mother?" Gandalf asked, not really wanting an answer that would involve her and Jess more with this woman and her family and their problems.

"I don't know," Lexi said. "But I think her disappearance might have something to do with my father."

Gandalf's expression probably matched the shocked look on Jess's face. Lexi stared at them both, her face flushed.

"Forget it," Lexi said. "I don't know what I'm talking about."

He was surprised when Evelyn offered to search with him and give him a tour of the trails. People on Azalea Court were more welcoming than he had expected, more openhearted than he had feared. Maybe not the woman next door looking to babysit only for white children, but everyone else.

Evelyn led him to the wooded path he remembered from the day before. This time Imani was awake, smiling and babbling at Evelyn.

"Do you have kids?" he asked.

Evelyn nodded. "A son in Brooklyn. Two grandchildren, grown out of the delightful baby years though. How old is she?"

"Almost four months. Her name is Imani."

"Lovely. Does it mean something?"

Why did people always ask that? Does Susan mean something, or Robert? Well, maybe they do, but no one asks about it. He pushed his annoyance down as Winda had taught him. "It means *faith* in Swahili. It is her grandmother's name. In Kenya children are named to honor the older generation."

"Are you from Kenya?" Evelyn asked.

"My wife is. Winda." He laughed. "That means *warrior!*"

Evelyn laughed too. "Thanks for the warning."

She pointed to a trail forking to the right. "That goes to the college. If you cross the athletic fields, there's a bridge and then you're on campus. It's the quickest way to get into town. But I've never seen Iris walk that way, so we'll skip it."

"Interesting. Winda starts teaching at the college in January, so maybe she can walk to work. In nice weather, anyway."

"We use these trails year-round, to walk and ski and snowshoe. And that trail," she pointed to a small path leading down to the river, "goes down along the riverbank. But it's narrow and too steep for Iris." She touched Timothy's shoulder. "This is a really nice community. I hope your family is happy here."

He pointed to the left, across the brown cornfields and grassy meadow. "Tell me about the state hospital. I saw the bench dedicated to people buried here but I didn't have time to read the plaque before the rain. Why are people buried out in a field, with no stones or anything?"

"Those are patients with no family to claim their bodies," she said. "Or too ashamed to claim them. There are several hundred people buried in that field. There's a program tomorrow morning at the Memorial Garden, if you want to learn more about the state hospital. Lots of folks living here have old connections to the place, and memories."

"What kind of memories?" Timothy asked, though he wasn't sure he wanted to know the answer.

"Like Dr. Blum, the husband of the missing woman," she said. "He was the head shrink and ran the place for the last forty years it was open."

"He must have some stories to tell."

Evelyn shook her head. "He doesn't talk about it much, though I hear he's writing a book. He's supposed to speak at the Memorial tomorrow, but who knows if he will now, with Iris missing. And I guess you know that our little circle of houses was originally built as housing for hospital staff. My mother-in-law was an attendant at the hospital. She bought our house with money deducted from her paycheck every week. Of course, Dr. Blum was probably *given* his as part of the job."

Timothy heard the resentment in her voice, hinting at a history he didn't think he wanted to know about. He looked down at Imani, who had fallen asleep with her pinkie finger in her mouth, her comfort of choice if her mother's breast wasn't available. They climbed a steep hill along the burial ground and came to the small park with the plaque.

"I must rest, catch my breath for a minute," Evelyn said, sitting on the stone bench.

Timothy looked across the fields. Their cluster of houses was visible on the hill beyond the mostly bare trees. Two women wearing shorts and tee shirts ran by them waving a greeting. He sat down next to Evelyn, who turned to face him.

Uh oh, he thought. He knew that look, when someone was going to share something you'd just as soon not know. Growing up in an odd-ball cult taught him early to keep his stories to himself and not judge others. He wished Winda were here. She was good with people, listening to their troubles and knowing just what to say to make them feel better. Still, this woman had been so kind to him.

"Do you believe in ghosts?" Evelyn asked.

Totally not what he expected. "I don't know. Not really, I guess. But Winda grew up in a culture in which people feel tied to their ancestors. Not ghosts, exactly. More like wise elders. They're always around, kind of available when you need them." He looked at Evelyn. "Why do you ask?"

"Since Iris went missing I've been feeling like this place—which I've never liked, for what it's worth—is erupting and spewing memories I can't get rid of. I can't stop thinking about the people who lived here, the long-gone people buried out there." She waved her hand across the frozen field.

"In my brain," she said, "the dead patients are swarming around. And I can't stop thinking about what happened to me. I was assaulted here, decades ago. It broke me, but I put it away. Now it's all flooding back and choking me. It's hard to breathe."

GLORIA

When Gloria heard the syncopated footsteps—cane, foot, foot—coming up from the basement, she poured a fresh mug of coffee. Iris looked scrubbed clean despite still wearing yesterday's rumpled clothes, but her face wore an expression of profound disorientation. She sat down, leaned her cane against the kitchen table, and hugged her pocketbook on her lap.

"Good morning," Gloria said. "Milk and sugar in your coffee?"

Iris nodded.

"You know, you don't need to carry your purse everywhere," Gloria said. "We're alone here and safe until three this afternoon when the kids get home from school. We've got to be out of here by then."

"I need to take my pills." Iris's voice trembled. "I have no clean clothes. I didn't even pack fresh underwear. I shouldn't use my credit card and don't have much cash, just what was left in my grocery jar. What was I thinking? I'm usually a planner, but this, well, this just shook me up so badly."

Gloria handed her the coffee. "This will help."

Iris sipped. She touched the vase of cut flowers on the red checked tablecloth. "These help too. Thank you." She turned to Gloria. "How could I leave with no plan other than getting away from Asher? And now the police are out looking for me with dogs. So stupid."

"Is there anyone you can call?"

"My daughter would probably help without telling anyone. But I left my phone at home." She cradled her purse in her lap, rocking it like a baby.

"You can use the phone here," Gloria said.

Tears flooded Iris's cheeks. Gloria handed her a tissue.

"I'm sorry, dear. You're being so nice to me. And I can't believe what I've done. I don't know how to go forward."

"You'll figure it out," Gloria said. She spoke from hard experience. "What can I get you to eat? Toast? Eggs? You must be ravenous."

"Yes. Thank you. But first I need my pills." Iris pushed aside the thick wad of papers in her purse, rattling the pill bottles at the bottom of the bag and lining them up on the table.

Gloria pointed at the bottles. "Are you ill?"

Iris looked thoughtful. "I don't think so. A few weeks ago, I discovered something horrible my husband did many years ago. I said angry things. I even threatened him with exposure. The next night I noticed that one of my heart pills was different. Asher is a doctor, and he said the pills were the same, just a different brand. But they weren't the same. They made me confused and wobbly, and I couldn't think straight."

"You don't seem confused now," Gloria said.

"Not anymore. You don't think I kept taking those new pills, do you? But I was confused and, well, heartbroken." Iris dabbed at her eyes with the tissue, then dug in her purse for a scrap of paper which she shook in the air. "I found the substitute pills in Asher's pharmacology book that's got pictures and looked them up. They're used to sedate people. I refilled my old prescription and stopped taking the new ones. I pretended to be confused so Asher wouldn't know. It was hard to believe my Asher would do that to me, but I had to accept that he did. That's when I started thinking about leaving."

Gloria read the paper and handed it back to Iris. "These are hardly ever prescribed these days. They have terrible side-effects."

"Are you a nurse?"

Gloria hesitated. "I used to be," she finally said.

Iris reached across the table for Gloria's hand. "How did you end up living in your car? I don't mean to pry or give offense. But I'm curious. You've been so good to me."

Gloria tried to calm her breathing. She stood up and poured more coffee. "Are you ready for some breakfast?" she asked.

"Yes," Iris said. "Thank you."

Making toast and scrambling eggs were ordinary things, but precious when you couldn't do them anymore. Gloria's meals were take-out when she was lucky, sometimes free food at one of the churches. She regularly dined from the tasting tables at Costco. She called them tapas for the desperate. What would she do when her parents' membership card expired next month? Sometimes—and her face blazed to think about this—she resorted to table scraps from the dumpsters behind restaurants.

She placed two plates on the table, one in front of Iris and one for herself. She sat down and sniffed deeply. "Smells so good, doesn't it," she said.

"Wonderful," Iris agreed.

Gloria forced herself to eat slowly, to taste every bite. When her father was sick, she fed him small forkfuls of scrambled eggs, the last solid food he could manage.

"I was a nurse," Gloria said. "I went to college in California and worked there for years. Not sure why I came back east. I applied for a job at the state hospital, but my mother freaked out about me working there. Too dangerous, she said, so I took a job in a nursing home. Three years ago, my mother got sick and I quit my job to take care of her. She died, and then my father started failing." She paused. "My mother turned into a sour old woman, but I adored my dad."

She hadn't minded leaving her job, hadn't minded doing round-the-clock care for two old sick people. It had felt right to wash them and feed them. Full circle of life and all that.

"What a good person you are to take care of them like that."

"My parents adopted me," Gloria said. "They chose me. I was glad to be able to repay their kindness." Glad, but it didn't turn out well. After her father's death she learned that there was no money. Their home, where she had lived for six years of caregiving, was heavily mortgaged.

"My father died in my arms eight months ago," Gloria said. "Wrapped in that old comforter I keep in my car."

Iris smiled. "You bundled me up in that too. Green vines and faded peach roses. Worn and well-loved."

"After he died, the bank took the house and I moved into my car," Gloria said. "I hadn't worked as a nurse—not outside my parents' home—for several years and couldn't afford to renew my nursing license."

"I'm so sorry." Iris patted Gloria's hand. "We're both in bad shape, aren't we?"

Gloria forced a laugh. "We are. But we can stay here for a few hours and eat as much as we want. My friend is kind, but her husband doesn't like me. We have to figure out our next step."

"I have no clue what to do," Iris said. "Shall we call Lexi?"

Gloria had mixed feelings about that plan. The daughter might be more concerned with getting her mother home than with helping her escape her life. But there weren't a lot of options. "Sure. Maybe your daughter can help. Do you want to use my friend's phone?"

Iris shook her head hard. "No, they'll be able to trace the call back here, won't they? That could get your friend in trouble, maybe lead back to you. Do pay phones even exist these days?"

"A few. There's one at the library. We'll head over there after lunch."

"But we're just eating breakfast."

Gloria laughed. "Welcome to my life! When I have a comfortable place and free food, I stay as long as I'm welcome and eat as much as is offered. After lunch we'll call your daughter and maybe check out the basement that I was telling you about."

"If I ever go home," Iris said, patting Gloria's hand. "If I still have a home after all this, you have a place to stay until you get back on your feet. As long as it takes."

Gloria squeezed Iris's hand. "Whatever happens, it's good to not be alone."

DETECTIVE McPHEE

She knew that her intuitive methods were sometimes the butt of jokes back at the station, but who cared as long as she got results? Still, she was a bit embarrassed about sitting on the front porch of Number Two Azalea Court, in one of the twin pink Adirondack rocking chairs, contemplating an imaginary conversation with the missing woman.

She looked at the list in her notebook. There had been no answer when she knocked again on Number Six. From her porch seat she had a good view of that front door in case the owners returned or tried to sneak out. She didn't think there was anything to the hoodie report, but she prided herself in being thorough and following up on all leads.

With each passing hour, finding the missing woman alive and unharmed got less likely. By all reports Iris Blum had been a competent elderly woman, even if her husband's diagnosis of dementia was correct. She probably didn't deserve to end a long life like this. Damn, here she was, thinking of Mrs. Blum in that pesky past tense. You slipped into it so easily, and it never failed to undo the people left behind after an accident. Or whatever this was.

She wasn't ready to give up on Mrs. Blum, not yet. She would conjure her up, picture the woman right next to her, in the matching pink rocker. The missing woman would be wearing a blue hooded jacket zipped tight against the November morning chill.

"Good morning, Iris," McPhee said quietly. "May I call you Iris?"

"Certainly, dear."

"We're doing everything we can to help you."

"Thank you. I do appreciate your efforts."

"Is there anything you'd like to share with me? Off the record? Any clues to help me find you?"

Imaginary Iris half-smiled. "What if I don't want to be found? Will you still help me?"

McPhee sat up straight. What if, indeed?

"What do you think happened to your mother?" Gandalf had asked in the garden.

"I think her disappearance might have something to do with my father."

Lexi couldn't believe she'd said that. Did she really believe that her father was somehow responsible?

The three women stood among waist-high vegetable stalks, brittle and broken. Gandalf's face turned the pale color of the dead vegetation. She took her girlfriend's hand and Lexi could tell Gandalf wished she were anywhere but there.

Lexi wished she could take back her accusatory words. She listened to the crisp flapping of plastic and pictured her mother huddled sick in that makeshift shelter or lying frozen next to the Mill River she loved in warmer weather.

"Don't mind me. I'm so upset I don't know what I'm saying," Lexi fumbled with her hat, pulling it over her ears. She returned to the path, searching her brain for something to say to change the mood. "You know, all this used to be the kitchen garden for the state hospital to feed patients?" She looked at the blank faces of her neighbors and walked ahead. "Well, let's finish this up."

They returned to their careful walk-and-look, settling into an uncomfortable silence as they turned down the last path. Jess got a phone call and gestured that she had to take it. She excused herself to walk ahead and have her conversation. There wasn't much left to investigate anyway. No more makeshift greenhouses or plastic covered structures.

It felt hopeless. Lexi started thinking about what if they never found her mother, what if she just disappeared, when Gandalf spoke.

"So," Gandalf said. "What kind of work do you do?"

Lexi wasn't expecting chitchat from Gandalf, who had a reputation on the Court as awkward and socially stiff. Lexi's parents didn't gossip, but Eric next door mentioned that Gandalf had testified in some kind of big government investigation, a scandal involving Homeland Security. Whatever the reason, she and her girlfriend—both tall and thin with cropped gray hair—kept to themselves. Lexi couldn't remember Gandalf ever speaking to her before other than a short greeting or necessary response.

"It's okay if you would rather not talk," Gandalf said into the silence.

Lexi smiled at her. "No, it's fine. You just surprised me. I'm a landscape architect. I design outdoor spaces, plantings and trees. I got my graduate degree from the Conway School over on Village Hill Road. In their old place, though, before they moved here."

Gandalf looked thoughtful. "Does your training affect how you look at these gardens, as a professional?"

Interesting woman, Lexi thought. She'd been thinking about the garden layout as they walked. "Professionally, I rarely use symmetry or grids," she said. She realized her father had never asked her a single question about her work.

"What about you?" she asked Gandalf. "What do you do?"

"I used to conduct mathematical research into hurricane behavior, creating models and formulas to explain how they act. But I left the university and am trying to write a book."

"About hurricanes?"

Gandalf nodded. She stopped to poke a pile of leaves and brush with a long stick.

Lexi frowned. Gandalf couldn't possibly think Iris was in there, could she?

"What about Jess?" she asked. "What does she do?"

Gandalf looked uncomfortable. She glanced at Jess, still on her phone, and tossed the long stick into the brush pile.

"She is a literature professor at the college," Gandalf said, and then hesitated.

Lexi imagined the woman trying to figure out what came next in an ordinary conversation.

Gandalf looked relieved when they reached the end of the row. "I guess we should go back and report to the policewoman. It doesn't appear that your mother is in the garden." She waved at Jess and pointed back towards the house.

Lexi hated to give up, but Gandalf was right. There was no evidence of her mother in the pale shriveled growth.

Jess finished her conversation, and the three women walked silently back to Azalea Court. Gandalf and Jess hurried to their house with a small wave and smile. Lexi imagined their relief at not having to be in the presence of catastrophe. She meandered back to Number Two, not sure what new bit of nasty family history would come tumbling out of her father's mouth next. Detective McPhee was sitting on one of mother's porch rockers. She stood up as Lexi climbed the steps.

"Could we talk?" McPhee asked.

Lexi nodded.

"Not here." McPhee pointed to the Circle.

They sat side by side on the bench, both staring past the bungalows to the ridge of Mt. Tom beyond. Without looking at Lexi, McPhee asked quietly, "Why do *you* think your mother left?"

What could she say? What did the detective know about their family secrets? What *could* she know? Lexi didn't know any of this stuff until last night.

"I don't know," Lexi whispered.

"Could it have something to do with your dad?"

"Where is he?"

"Inside."

Lexi had never considered how it felt to air dirty family laundry, at

least not personally. She'd known people who hid shameful information to spare themselves the pain of facing it, but Lexi had never seen
her own family in that light. She wasn't sure she was ready to now.

"I don't know," she said again. "Have you found out anything?"

McPhee shook her head. "No. But I'm beginning to suspect this
wasn't a situation of a confused elderly woman just wandering off.
And I doubt that someone kidnapped her. I'm starting to wonder if
your mother could have left on purpose, to escape something. Until we
know what she needed to escape, it'll be pretty impossible to find her.
To help her."

ERIC GOLDEN

Standing in his front yard, Eric looked at each house around the Court. Who knew what really went on behind your neighbors' closed doors? How well could you know other people, even living so physically close for years? Some days he felt like he barely knew his own wife, and clearly, he didn't know Asher very well even though he considered the old guy a good friend.

He was not being a good friend. He should be by Asher's side, offering support and unquestioning companionship, rather than avoiding him and gossiping with the neighbors. He should go there right now. Asher was probably alone, since his daughter was deep in conversation with the detective on the Circle bench. Eric waved at them as he walked by and climbed the steps to Number Two.

Asher opened the door before Eric knocked.

"I messed up," Asher said, stepping back so Eric could enter.

That phrase again. Doubly surprising from the usually reticent old guy.

"What do you mean?" Eric asked.

Asher sat in Iris's chair, another surprise. Eric sat in Asher's chair, stared at the subtly patterned rug, and waited. The man looked awful; the dark circles always present under his deep-set eyes seemed to be growing deeper and wider, huge pools of gray sorrow.

"I did some bad things," Asher finally said. "Iris found out about them, and now Lexi is finding out too."

"What kind of bad things?"

"Things I had to do, to take care of my family," Asher said. "I had to protect Iris from her friend who was destroying our future. The fifties were a dangerous time for Jews. I am responsible for Iris's friend Harriet losing her job and going to prison. I ruined Harriet's life, and now she's dead. I was dishonest with Iris, and now she hates me."

Eric didn't know how to respond. He had never heard Asher speak like this, words tumbling out of his chest with such sad force. What was it about Iris's disappearance that made his neighbors start revealing their long-buried secrets?

"I'm not a monster," Asher continued. "I didn't sleep easily after the things I did. Do I have regrets? Yes, of course. Would I do it again? I believe I would. Does that make me a bad person?"

Asher looked like he wanted to say more. Eric waited, but nothing more came. How could he make Asher feel less awful?

"You're a Holocaust survivor," Eric said. "Right?"

"Yes, as a teenager. A child."

"Maybe that explains what you did? Because of what you lived through? Your fears about bad things happening to your family again?"

"No." Asher sighed deeply. "You don't understand. That's why I should have known better. Acted better. *Tikkun olam*."

"What's that?"

"It's Hebrew, means to repair the world. That's what Jews are supposed to do. Not make it worse."

Eric leaned over to awkwardly pat Asher's shoulder. What else could he say? He had no vocabulary to respond to this kind of thing—in either Hebrew or English. He wished he knew the right words to offer comfort. But he suspected there were no words and no comfort available for Asher.

Asher stood up. "Thank you for listening. Please go now. I need to think. To remember."

Eric walked to the door, then turned back. He touched Asher's shoulder again. "I don't blame you, for what you did."

"I blame myself," Asher said.

ASHER BLUM

After Eric left, Asher leaned against the door. His legs felt heavy with ancient memories, weak with regret, and barely able to carry him to Iris's chair. He closed his eyes, and let the old pictures come.

He and Iris had been married and living on Azalea Court for three years when things fell apart. It was 1956. They were happy together, although he understood vaguely that he was more content than she was. He had his work—important work, work that mattered—and she wasn't entirely satisfied with being a homemaker. But things would improve for her when the baby was born. She was nearing the end of the first trimester and glowed in a way she hadn't since he extricated her from her Brooklyn life.

That morning he kissed her goodbye at the door and enjoyed the October colors as he walked to his office at the state hospital. He was in a good mood, anticipating the afternoon meeting with the hospital trustees at which he would present the excellent statistics for the past six months of electroshock therapy. Ruth Smith, his secretary, met him with a cup of tea and the morning newspaper, and he settled at his desk to begin the day.

"You have a visitor," Ruth announced twenty minutes later. "No appointment, but she insists it's critically important that she see you. Says her name is Harriet Sarnoff."

Asher forgot to breathe. If it had been under his control his heart would have stopped beating as well. He tried to speak, but his lips were frozen. He nodded to Ruth who escorted Harriet into his office then left and closed the door. He pointed to the wooden chair facing his desk. Harriet did not sit. She paced the width of his office, back and forth three or four times without looking at him. Then she stood in front of his desk. She leaned both hands on the polished wooden edge and stared at him.

"Harriet." His voice was shaky. He tried to steady it. "What do you want?"

"I want my life back. The life you stole from me."

He shook his head. "I didn't steal anything."

Harriet reached into her purse and took out a folded paper. "It took some doing, getting a copy of the letter you wrote to the principal of my school." She waved it in his face. "But now I have proof. Proof that you got me fired. With the information you sent him, the principal contacted the FBI, which led to me being called before the Senate committee."

"Please," he said. "Keep your voice down."

Her voice rose in volume in response. "You are the reason I spent six months in prison. Because of you, I'll never get another job as a teacher or a chemist!"

She was yelling now. Her face was red, her hair escaping its barrette. "You stole my best friend, and you stole my livelihood!"

Ruth opened the door a crack. "Everything okay in here, Dr. Blum?"

"Thank you, Ruth. It's fine." When the door was closed, he turned to Harriet. "Please calm down. We can work this out."

"I will not be calm, and there's nothing to work out." Spittle sprayed from her mouth onto his desk. "I'm taking this to the local newspaper. I'm sure they'll be interested in the activities of their respected psychiatrist, a man trusted with the mental health of so many suffering people." She reached back and undid the barrette, letting her hair spring free, then shook her head hard, making the curls whip the air. He recognized the gesture from the few political meetings he attended with Harriet and Iris on campus, before he realized their danger.

He stared at her. She looked like a wild-woman—which was probably what she wanted—and for a moment he was frightened. He wasn't that worried about the newspaper. After all, Harriet *was* a Communist so she got what she deserved, and the local paper would see it his way. But Iris? Iris would never forgive him. His wife would leave him, take their baby, and go back to Brooklyn with Harriet. He couldn't let that happen. He studied Harriet's face, deep scarlet now, her hair Medusa-like around her face.

"What do you think about that, Dr. Rat? How'd you like everyone in your town to know what you did to me?" She paused then and rubbed her wet cheeks. For a second or two the fury receded, and she looked profoundly sad. "Do you have any idea what it's like to be in prison?"

He hadn't noticed the tears before that moment, and he felt sorry for her. She wasn't a bad person, not really. Not mentally ill either, just unhinged by her sorrow. Maybe he could persuade her to leave quietly and never return. "Harriet," he began, but something in his tone seemed to enrage her further.

She grabbed the vase of artificial flowers on his desk, dumped the fake lilies of the valley on the floor, and lifted the vase over her head.

He stared at her. She wouldn't physically attack him, would she? Reaching under his desk, he pushed the panic button.

Harriet slammed the vase on the edge of his desk. Better than my head, he thought, jerking back from the flying fragments of painted porcelain.

In less than a minute two white-coated attendants rushed into his office. Asher's thoughts ricocheted between satisfaction that the emergency system worked the way it was supposed to and horror at the rapid cascade of events. Unstoppable and inevitable and escalating events.

"Restrain her," he ordered, struggling to control his voice. "She attacked me. Give her Thorazine 100 mg IM stat."

The attendants grabbed Harriet's arms and pulled her away from Asher's desk. One man covered her mouth with his large hand, cutting off her curses and threats. As they pushed Harriet toward the office door, she wriggled one arm free and socked the attendant, who was so surprised he released his grip on her mouth.

"You will regret this until the day you die," Harriet said, her voice low and deadly calm. Then she was silenced, immobilized, and dragged out of the office.

Asher nudged her purse underneath his desk with his foot and slipped the copy of his letter into his top drawer.

Ruth watched the procession down the hall to the south wing and handed Asher a clipboard with the necessary forms. "I'm sorry, Dr. Blum," she said. "I should have realized she was dangerous."

"No way you could have known," Asher said. "I believe she has a history of paranoia and violence, but she presented as a reasonable woman. Until she turned on me." He took the clipboard. "We'd better admit her. I'll take care of the paperwork."

Ruth nodded. "I'll get someone to clean up this mess."

She closed the door, leaving him in silence. He brushed the pottery shards off his desk chair and collapsed onto it, then took a tissue from the decoupage box Iris made for his office. He wiped the speckles of Harriet's spit off the polished desktop and turned his attention to the commitment paperwork.

Sixty-some years later, Asher could still picture the spit spots on his desk. Could remember being unable to draw a breath. What he did to Harriet was wrong. He knew that. He accepted it and had tried to minimize the pain his actions caused much as he could. He paid for Harriet's upkeep at the hospital and personally managed her medications. He visited her every week on the women's locked ward, although she never once acknowledged his presence. He sat by her bedside at the hospital after her stomach was pumped when she managed to stockpile her Thorazine tablets and take them all late one February night, almost succeeding in ending her life. He held her hand as she gained consciousness, even though she tried to bite his hand when she recognized him. After that, he increased her dose and switched to a liquid form.

When Harriet got pregnant two years into her time at the hospital, he tried unsuccessfully to find out if she had been raped or had consented, as if one could really consent on the drugs he'd prescribed for her. He arranged for good prenatal care and then for the little girl to be adopted. When Harriet succeeded in killing herself, he stood alone by the fresh mound of dirt at the burial ground. He recited the Hebrew prayer and whispered his apologies.

Of course, no one knew about any of this. Iris didn't even know Harriet was at the hospital until she went snooping in his private papers. Or maybe Iris *did* know, in her bones, because she lost their first baby two weeks after he had Harriet committed to the state hospital.

The one thing that wasn't in the files, the one thing he kept out of all the records and never told a soul, was about Harriet's little girl. He monitored her progress, made sure that her adoptive parents were doing well by her, once even watched her on the elementary school playground. He lost track of the young woman when she went out west to college.

Some nights when he had trouble sleeping, Asher wondered about the child. Did she know anything about her birth mother? Would she try one day to contact her birth family? He thought of her as a niece or distant cousin and considered trying to meet her. She would be a couple of years older than Lexi.

But what good would meeting her do? What good would any of it do?

None of these things could ever atone for his actions against Harriet, against Iris. How could he try to explain, to beg Iris for forgiveness, if she wasn't here to listen?

EVELYN TURNER

This might not be such a good idea, but that rarely stopped Evelyn from forging ahead. She knocked on the door of Number Four hoping that Jess would answer, not that prickly woman with the silly wizard name. She was in luck.

"Hello, Evelyn," Jess said.

"Do you have a minute to talk?" Evelyn asked.

Jess stepped back to let Evelyn enter. "Sure."

When they were seated, Evelyn had second thoughts. She didn't know Jess well at all. "I'm sorry to bother you," she began, "but you're on the committee for the Memorial Garden dedication tomorrow, aren't you?"

"I am. I'm the MC, but only because no one else was willing to do it."

"Can you tell me what to expect at the program?"

Jess grimaced. "It's sort of up in the air right now because of Mrs. Blum being missing. Dr. Blum was the main speaker."

Oh joy, Evelyn thought. "What's he supposed to speak about?"

"His book, I gather. The one he's writing about the state hospital and the history of the treatment of mental illness over the last couple of centuries." Jess reached for a stack of papers on the coffee table. "If it helps, the title of his book, and also of his talk, is *What We Thought We Knew.*"

At least he admitted to some uncertainty, Evelyn thought.

"May I ask why you want to know?"

"Just curious," Evelyn said. "Will there be an opportunity for people in the community to speak?"

Jess nodded. "A few people have asked to speak in memory of family members who were patients at the hospital or to read poems." She hesitated. "Do you want to speak? I could put you on the program."

"Oh, no no no." Evelyn stood up. "I'm not even sure I'm going to attend. I really like Iris, but I can't stand Dr. Blum. When something horrible happened to me many years ago at his precious hospital, he wouldn't help. He was horrible."

Evelyn covered her face with her hands. Why was she blurting like this to a stranger? She was out of control recently, ever since Iris went missing—thinking about dead patients and wandering ghosts. She couldn't seem to keep her mouth shut. She had better get home.

Jess reached a hand to touch Evelyn's shoulder, but Evelyn pulled away.

"I'm sorry," Evelyn said. "Please forget what I said. I'm just upset about Iris."

JESS SIMON

Standing in the open doorway, Jess watched Evelyn hurry back across the Circle to her house.

"What was that about?" Gandalf stood behind Jess, wrapped her arms around her, and nuzzled her neck.

"I have no clue. She wanted to know about the ceremony tomorrow, but I have no idea why. And then she started talking about hating Dr. Blum. About something that happened to her at the hospital when he was in charge."

"What happened to her?" Gandalf asked.

"She didn't say. And then she ran home. She seemed very upset."

"Strange," Gandalf said.

"People are strange," Jess agreed. "And unhappy."

"Not us, of course."

Jess thought about that. Were they happy? Neither one of them had wanted to leave Manhattan, but it had seemed necessary for Gandalf's mental stability. After testifying against the federal agents who kidnapped and interrogated her, Gandalf felt powerful for a few days, then became terrified that they would be back to kill her. They tried moving to another apartment, even got married and Gandalf took Jess's last name. Finally, they gave up and left the city.

Jess reached under Gandalf's sweater for the gold wizard charm she had given her beloved, warm from Gandalf's skin, and kissed it.

"Love you, wizard," she whispered.

SATURDAY EARLY AFTERNOON

What We Thought We Knew:

The use of wet packs has been continued with excellent results. Many of the recent cases have had them daily, for periods varying from one to several weeks. Fifty-eight cases have been treated, with favorable results in all except two, who could not bear them well. . . . The effect is quieting, so that very often the patient goes to sleep while in the pack.

—John A Houston,
Northampton State Hospital Annual Report, 1900

THE WOMEN

Saturday afternoon was chilly and raw. Our emotions perfectly matched the weather.

Iris had been missing for more than twenty-four hours. We knew from television cop shows that after that point the chances of a missing person being found alive went way down. A few of us googled it, to check out the statistics. Turned out the twenty-four hours was most accurate for missing children, but the statistics still weren't good, and it didn't make us feel any better.

Those Azalea Court residents who had joined the search party felt particularly despondent. We had entertained cinematic hopes of being part of a joyful discovery, a celebratory rescue, an emotional reunion of an old woman with her family. Finding nothing and seeing little police presence on the Court made us feel even more sad and demoralized.

Many of us began to feel that the situation was hopeless. Iris was lost to us. We wished we had been better friends to her. Once we heard she was sick, we could have brought casseroles, offered to spend time with her, maybe read aloud her favorite classic novels. We could have accompanied her on her daily walks by her beloved Mill River. Some of us shared these regrets with each other and started talking to each other as if we might become friends as well as neighbors.

Our selfishness accused us. Shamed us. We resolved to be better in the future. Be better friends, stronger allies for each other.

GLORIA

After lunch and a second shower, just because it felt so good to be clean, Gloria helped Iris into the nest of sleeping bags and blankets in the back of the Subaru wagon. Their bellies were full, and they had a plan: drive to the library and call Lexi from the pay phone. Gloria draped the worn quilt around Iris's shoulders, running her finger along the spring-green leaves and faded roses. She tucked her garbage bag of clothes between the old woman and the back window. As she went to close the back door, a sob from the faded roses stopped her.

"What is it? What's wrong?" Gloria asked.

Iris wiped her eyes. "You are being so kind to me. I'm not used to such warmth from people. And I feel like I've known you forever."

"I feel that way too," Gloria said.

"I'm sad because I'm thinking about my friend Harriet and what my husband did to her. I know that Harriet's dead, but I don't know how she died. I don't know if anyone was kind to her. If she had something soft around her. If anyone held her at the end."

Gloria sat next to her and patted her hand. "I'm so sorry. What can I do?"

"Can we visit Harriet? At the burial grounds. To say goodbye?"

Gloria didn't know how to answer. It was probably a very bad idea.

"I know it's risky," Iris said. "But I need to go there. Please?"

"The cops might be keeping an eye on the place."

"Maybe, but I doubt they know anything about Harriet, or why I left, so hopefully they're not looking for me there."

It felt odd to park in her usual spot, as though weeks had passed instead of hours. Gloria insisted that Iris wear her new red plaid winter poncho from the free rack at the Survival Center rather than her own coat.

"They'll be looking for your blue hooded jacket," she explained.

The rain had ended overnight, and the temperature had plummeted. The fields sparkled with ice crystals in the afternoon sun. Iris leaned on her cane, and their walk to the burial ground was slow. Much of the old woman's energy seemed to have been drained from her body. Gloria worried about Iris's weariness. What would she do if Iris collapsed?

They arrived at the burial ground, grateful that they saw no one except three college-aged women running in skimpy track clothes. Iris and Gloria sank onto the stone bench and exchanged glances as the girls passed, chatting as they ran, apparently oblivious to the cold.

"Harriet is buried somewhere in that field. I think she'd like it here, actually. She'd especially like the dandelions when spring comes. When we were kids, we loved to blow dandelion seeds at each other. When I think of Harriet as a child, I picture her with those white feathery seeds in her eyelashes."

"Tell me about her."

"She loved hay fields. Loved the stunted shrub pines on our island and the huge fields of ferns. She liked maple trees too, but not the red ones. She preferred the golden leaves. And birches." Iris pointed across the field. "She'd love that stand of tall birches. I hope she can see it from where she's buried. I wish I knew her exact burial site."

"What did she look like?"

"Wild curly hair that never minded. A long thin face. Growing up, the mean kids called it horsey, but it wasn't really. It was strong. I don't know when her strength deserted her."

"Did she have mental illness?"

Iris shook her head. "I don't think so. She wrote me that she saw a counselor after she got out of prison. Said she felt unmoored. Lost. But was that mental illness, or just a reasonable response to awful things happening to her? I don't know."

"If she wasn't mentally ill, how did your husband have her committed?"

Iris made a sound that was half laugh, half sob. "All he had to do was scribble his name on a form. Maybe he had to get one of his shrink buddies to cosign, maybe a judge to okay it. There were few patient rights back then. No formal court hearings or full evaluations. My Asher was God."

"I'm so sorry." Gloria took Iris's hand. "When's the last time you saw her?"

"At my wedding. But we wrote letters, almost every day. I was so unhappy leaving Brooklyn, and I hated it here. Asher wasn't much help. He tried to pay attention to me, but he was completely involved in his work. The only things that kept me afloat were Harriet's letters. I got a box at the post office under my maiden name and Asher never knew. After Harriet was released from prison, I begged her to move here." Iris's voice cracked. "But she had no use for Asher. I didn't know then that my husband was the reason she lost her job and went to prison. She didn't tell me, to spare my feelings I suppose. If only I knew. If only she had come here. We kept writing, less frequently after she was released from prison, and then one day in 1956 the letters stopped. I was frantic."

"Did you try to search for her?"

"Of course. I called everyone who might know her—friends from school and our families in Maine. I even called the police department in Brooklyn, the missing persons department. No one knew anything."

"When did you find out she was a patient at the hospital?"

Iris turned to face Gloria, her face glistening. "About a month ago. From Asher's papers." She patted her purse, stuffed with a folded stack of yellowed pages. "He kept them in his desk in his study. In *my* house. How can I ever forgive that? How can I ever forgive the things he did to her?"

"I can't imagine forgiving him. You must hate him now."

Iris shook her head. "I don't know what I feel."

They sat in silence for a few moments.

"Do you feel any better, sitting here where Harriet is buried?"

Iris sniffled. "Not really. I dreamed about her last night. I could see her so clearly. She was trying to tell me something, but I couldn't grasp it and then I woke up and she was gone. Now, I can't feel her at all. Not here; she's not here. It's like she died and left me all over again, and I can't bear thinking of her dead and alone.

Gloria took her hand. "Maybe she's not alone. Have you noticed the old, hand-lettered sign on the river trail for Rebecca's Way? I don't know who Rebecca is, or was, but maybe she was here the same time as your Harriet. I'd like to believe they were friends."

DETECTIVE McPHEE

The reprimand was unexpected and unfair. McPhee stood in front of her supervisor's desk and concentrated on keeping her face empty of expression.

"Is there a *reason* you haven't followed up with the report of a stranger in a hoodie in the neighborhood, Detective?"

"Not yet, sir. Stranger involvement doesn't seem that likely. I've been trying to interview a neighbor who wears a hoodie, but she has not been available. Our investigation now suggests possible involvement by the husband."

"Do you know who Dr. Blum is?"

McPhee nodded, but inside she seethed. Treating important people differently than ordinary citizens was one of her least favorite parts of police work. Her supervisor was hyper-aware of the town power structure, always reminding officers to be respectful of the public, especially those with money and clout.

"Tread very carefully, Detective. This could become a high-profile case. People are frightened and demanding results. The citizen who reported a person wearing a hoodie deserves to have his concern looked into, even if he refused to give his name. *Your* job is to follow up every single possible lead immediately. Do you understand that?"

McPhee tried to ignore the waves of exhaustion flooding her body. Exhaustion and shame at being summoned from the field and spoken to like a rookie. Had she missed something important? Was her working theory totally off base? Or was this another example of her supervisor's bias against female cops? She would head back to Azalea Court now and go over all her notes again.

"Yes, sir. I'll look into it right away."

LEXI BLUM

Despite the raw chill outside, Lexi couldn't stand being in the cottage with her shell of a father. She made him lunch and started a load of his laundry, then escaped to the front porch, pulling her mother's rocking chair into the weakly sunny spot at the front edge.

Detective McPhee's theory about her mother escaping from her home left Lexi with a clenched stomach. Probably because the detective's theory mirrored her own impossible thoughts. She watched McPhee drive onto the Court about two o'clock and park her car. The detective didn't get out right away but sat leaning on the steering wheel staring at a small notebook. When she did climb out of the car, there was something different, less confident, in her gait. She waved at Lexi and walked toward Number Six. Why did the detective want to talk with Arnie and Aggie again, when she'd already interviewed them like everyone else?

By then, her mother had been gone over twenty-four hours and waiting for someone to find her was more intolerable with each passing hour. Over and over, Lexi reviewed her relationship with her mother and wished they had been closer. Why hadn't they been the kind of mother and daughter who share intimate details and random thoughts? If they'd been closer, maybe she would have a better idea of what prompted this, of where to search for her. Or maybe, if the detective was correct, to understand *why* her mother might not want to be found.

Lexi couldn't think clearly. Her thoughts spiraled, then wandered, then twisted themselves in knots. But one idea kept recurring: Harriet. Somehow, this had to be about Harriet. Her father was the only one who could fully explain that. Lexi knew he hadn't told her the whole story, because it didn't all make sense. Yet. She knew she had to force him to tell her the rest of it—however awful it was and however little she wanted to hear it and however much he resisted. It felt like the only way to find her mother.

She walked back inside her parents' home and stood in front of her father. She was almost undone when she saw him sitting in her mother's chair and cradling her knitting basket. Lexi steeled herself and did what she had to.

"Dad. If we're going to find Mom before it's too late, I need to know everything. No more half-truths. No more stories about Jewish partisans in the forest eighty-some years ago. What happened a month ago? What happened yesterday?"

He was silent, sitting like a man carved from granite. She wondered if he was going to ignore her entirely. When he began to speak, his voice was weedy with sorrow.

"I'm not proud of this," he said. "I believed that Harriet threatened Iris and me building a good life together. So, I wrote that letter and mailed it. That one thing led to the rest of it."

He told her everything. At least, she hoped it was everything. He talked about getting Harriet fired and arrested, about her visit to Northampton, about committing her to the hospital. Tears pooled under his eyes when he described Harriet's pregnancy and arranging her daughter's adoption and the suicide attempt and finally her death. He didn't try to justify anything. It was the saga of a man's actions and his shame.

She didn't interrupt, probably couldn't have spoken to stop a murder. As she listened, those knots in her brain snaked down her air pipe into her lungs, making it painful to breathe. When he finished, she concentrated on sucking air in and pushing it out, wishing she hadn't flunked yoga.

When she could finally speak, she asked, "How could you, one person, have someone committed to the hospital? Wasn't there a court-mandated evaluation or something?"

"Not really. We were hopelessly overcrowded in 1956. It was the peak of patient census. The laws changed later, but back then a physician affirmed the patient's mental illness with his signature. The rest was pretty much just paperwork."

"Did Mom know all this?"

He shook his head. "Not until recently."

"About a month ago, right? When she started acting so strange?"

"October 10," he said. "I'll never forget the date. I left the house as usual that afternoon at four-thirty to take my constitutional."

Her father was such a creature of habit. Every afternoon, two miles walking the roads of what was once his kingdom, now transformed into an ordinary neighborhood of apartments, houses, and condos.

"I came home an hour later, as usual, expecting to find her in the kitchen surrounded by smells of simmering soup with garden herbs and my martini on the table. But the kitchen was empty. Iris was in my office, sitting in my leather chair. She had apparently bitten her lip and there was a thin trail of blood to her chin. My papers covered her lap."

"She found the hospital records?"

He nodded. "I took a tissue from my desk and went to wipe her chin, but she slapped my hand away. She had never before touched me with anything other than love."

"What did she say?" I asked.

"Just three words, over and over: 'How could you?'"

"Good question. I want to know the answer too."

He shook his head. "She dragged it all up, brought all the old ugliness, the strife, into the open. Harriet had always been a pain in the ass, always telling Iris what to think and how to act. Starting on that god-forsaken island in Maine and then at college, even after I forbid Iris to have anything to do with her. Harriet's politics could have ruined us. In spite of my efforts, that woman lived with us our entire married life. She was an extra setting at the breakfast table. An accusing body between us in bed. Always shaking her bony finger at me."

Lexi was breathless again, those knots swelling in her lungs, taking up all the space.

Her father kept talking. "I told Iris I did what I had to. Your mother knows everything now. Well, everything except Harriet's baby. She doesn't know anything about that. I keep those files separately."

"You're still keeping secrets from her? I can't believe you!"

He wiped his eyes. "I know."

"What did she say, about it all?"

"She said what I did was unethical. Criminal."

"It was."

"True. But try to see it from my perspective, Lexi. Remember that the ink was not yet dry on my promotion when Harriet showed up. What choice did I have?"

"You could have been honest with your wife."

"That's what Iris said when she found the files. She shook her fist at me, saying she wouldn't let me get away with it. That she would go to the newspaper, to the police. I tried to reason with her. Harriet was long gone and what good would it do? I've never seen her so furious. She told me she *hated* me." His tone was surprised, almost argumentative, as if he were an attorney trying to convince a judge of his wife's unreasonable reaction.

Lexi wanted to throw up. It took all her concentration to keep the revulsion out of her voice. She might have failed, because her father's face fell into sorrow and his voice grew so small that she had to lean close to hear. "What did you do when she threatened you?"

"I substituted a pill that would make her confused, so she wouldn't be able to do those awful things. I gave her such a low dose; it couldn't possibly hurt her. I would never hurt Iris. I love her."

"She figured out about the pills? That's why she left?"

"Yes. I assume so. She left the bottle of pills on my desk and took my papers."

"I can't believe you did those things."

He rested his head on her mom's knitting basket, speaking through the yarn. "I can't either. That's not the kind of man I wanted to be. But what can I do now? Is there anything I can do to make it better?"

What could she say to him? Lexi left him there, hugging the jewel-tone yarn balls, and went back outside. She forgot her jacket but couldn't bear to return to his house to retrieve it.

Before that Saturday afternoon, Lexi had never understood how a person's whole life can change in a few moments. But that had just happened; her childhood was transformed, her family shattered.

ERIC GOLDEN

Sitting on an overturned metal bucket, Eric pulled weeds from the garden in front of Number One Azalea Court, tossing them on the pile of brittle-brown leaves and dead flowers in the wheelbarrow. Normally he liked the quiet of Saturdays when the kids played soccer and Bea wandered in the stores downtown. He liked the repetitive tasks of the fall garden clean-up, meditative in their simplicity. Cut back perennials, plant bulbs, pull weeds, gather leaves, repeat. It was a bonus that the work offered the best view of the goings-on around the Court, without seeming to be nosy. Today he would rather be doing something more to find Iris, but he had no idea how to help. If there was any help to offer. So instead, he pulled weeds.

He waved at Donnie, who was dressed for a run and stretching against his front stoop. He pretended not to notice Lexi sobbing on her parents' porch, telling himself he was giving her privacy, but knowing that he had no idea how to comfort her. He wondered what Detective McPhee was doing for such a long time inside Number Six. True that Aggie wore a hoodie, and the guy with the German Shepherd had reported seeing a hoodie-wearing person near Iris at the burial ground, but McPhee had been in there for almost an hour. When Bea pulled up with the kids, he was ready to move on to the next bungalow and trying to decide whether it would be more respectful to Asher to skip his house, or weed it, acting like nothing was different. Even when everything was different.

"We won two games, Dad!" Morgan shouted. "I made an awesome goal."

"Great," Eric said. "What about you, Marc?"

"I hate soccer," Marc mumbled, dragging himself up the steps and into the house.

Bea laughed. "He hates everything. Me most of all."

"You sound cheerful about it," Eric said.

"Adolescence," Bea said. "What's going on?" She pointed with her chin across the Circle, at Aggie walking towards them, flanked by the two detectives.

"Don't know," Eric said, standing up and moving to Bea's side.

McPhee called out to them. "Hello! We need to talk to your daughter again, please. Just a few questions."

Morgan moved closer to her mother. McPhee stepped forward, leaving Aggie with the other detective.

"When you came home from school yesterday, Morgan, did you stay in your house?"

Morgan shook her head.

"What did you do?" McPhee asked.

"I went to Aggie's house, to play with her dolls."

Bea shot a toxic look at Eric. "You let her do that?"

He frowned. "You were supposed to take the kids back to work with you. Instead, you just dropped them off without even checking to see if I was here."

"Where else would you be? You're the stay-at-home parent, remember?"

"With someone kidnapped from our street, you should have made sure," he said.

McPhee held up her hand to quiet them. "What time did you bring the children home?" she asked Bea, her voice calm.

"Quarter to three, maybe? I picked them up at school at two thirty and was back at work by three."

McPhee turned to Eric. "And when did you see Morgan?"

"I came home about four. Morgan arrived a couple of minutes later. You came over at about the same time and talked to both kids, remember?"

McPhee checked her notebook. "That's right, about four fifteen." She turned back to Morgan. "Were you with Aggie the whole time, from when your mom dropped you off until you came home and talked with me?"

"Yes."

"You're certain of that?"

Morgan nodded.

"Thank you. That's all for now." McPhee nodded to Aggie who turned to leave. Did Eric imagine the brief defiant glance that crossed her face?

"Do you know what happened to Mrs. Blum?" Morgan asked.

"No," McPhee said. "Not yet."

"Are the kids in danger? Should we keep them home?" Bea asked.

McPhee shrugged. "Being careful is probably a good idea until we figure out what happened. I'd keep the kids in the house for now."

"Is Aggie in trouble for playing with me?" Morgan asked.

"No," McPhee said. "Mrs. North isn't in trouble at all. Thanks to you."

GLORIA

"How do you feel about breaking the law?" Gloria asked Iris.

"I suppose it depends on which law."

"Well." Gloria waved her arm in a broad sweep over the burial ground. "This is all very moving and nostalgic, but it's not a good idea for you to be here. We need to call your daughter and then get you someplace safe to stay tonight while we figure out the next step."

"What does that have to do with breaking the law?"

"We may have to illegally enter that building I mentioned. Haskell." Gloria stood up and offered Iris her arm. "But one thing at a time. First, let's go call your daughter."

Fifteen minutes later at the library phone booth, Iris hesitated with her finger in the air above the numbers. She turned to Gloria.

"Why am I so nervous? She's my daughter. I know she'll help me."

"I wish I had a daughter. Call her."

Iris nodded, then punched in the phone number. The phone rang twice before Lexi answered.

"Lexi," Iris said. "Don't say my name. Are you alone?"

"Yes."

"Can you talk privately?"

"Yes. Yes. Are you okay?"

"I'm fine, dear. Where are you right now?"

"On your porch. Where are you?"

"I'm calling from a pay phone, so they can't trace my call."

"Pay phone? Do they still exist? Never mind that. Who's *they*? Is someone hurting you?"

"Oh, no, dear. No one took me or hurt me. It's such a very long story. But I need your help. And please, you can't tell your father or the police where I am."

"I think I know the story. At least, I know what Dad did." Her voice cracked and broke.

"Don't cry. We'll figure this out. Just please don't say anything to your father. Or the police. Promise me?"

"Of course. Can I come to you?"

"Not yet. I'm nowhere safe now." She turned to Gloria and asked, "What should I ask her to do?"

"Collect warm blankets, a flashlight, thermos bottles with hot tea. Tell her I'll call her tonight with our plan."

Iris relayed the instructions to her daughter, adding, "Bring me some clean underwear from my top dresser drawer too. I have to hang up now. Can you get that stuff together?"

"Of course, but why?"

"My friend will call you later and tell you where to meet me."

"Wait, don't hang up. What friend? This is nuts, Mom. You don't need to camp out. You can stay with me. Or, I'll get us a hotel room."

"Too risky. The police are probably watching you and I'm not ready to be found. I'm with a friend and I'm safe. I love you, dear." Iris placed the receiver on the hook but didn't let go. She felt frozen.

Gloria took Iris's hand off the receiver. "Are you okay? Won't your daughter help us?"

Iris roused herself to answer. "Of course, she will. It's me. I can't remember the last time I told Lexi I love her."

"Well," Gloria said, "you've told her now.

"Yes, and let's get away from here. I think I'm ready to break that law."

SATURDAY LATE AFTERNOON

What We Thought We Knew:

Shock treatment with methanol combined with insulin has been continued with what we believe to be encouraging results, although this form of treatment is far from being a specific one and may eventually be abandoned for something better.

—Arthur N. Ball,
Northampton State Hospital Superintendent Report,
1939

THE WOMEN

As it often does, the gloaming brought dark thoughts. We anticipated a second night of Iris being gone and most of us had no words for our feelings. They were all mixed up. Fear with excitement, worry with relief. We tried to go about our usual evening tasks—making food, eating, cleaning up, getting children to bed, pouring a glass of wine, selecting a book to read or a movie to watch—but our hearts weren't in it.

Some of us considered knocking on Asher's door to ask if he wanted company or needed anything. But his daughter was there, we reminded ourselves, so he wasn't alone. We sat closer on the sofa to our loved ones, made the goodnight hugs last longer than usual. We called our oldest friends long distance, even though we didn't really have much to say, just to hear the music of their absent voices. We thought about calling a neighbor, even though we rarely telephoned each other, because they would understand how creeped out we felt. Odd how it takes something awful to bring us together, we mused. To finally really notice each other.

How could something like this happen on our familiar, even boring, Azalea Court, we wondered. What difference would Iris's disappearance make to her neighbors, if she was not found? Would we keep trying to find our missing friend, or just return to our individual lives?

DONNIE TURNER

Donnie stared at Evelyn's back, her muscles stiff and unyielding through her sweater. They ate an early dinner. Then Evelyn simmered his favorite chicken stew with mushrooms and carrots and dill for the next day. Probably because she was planning to do something awful at the memorial park dedication the next morning. Evelyn had a habit of being really thoughtful and sweet before acting in a way she knew he would hate. He thought of it as an inoculation of niceness, like giving a vaccine to prevent his anger or disappointment at her actions to come.

Despite the stew, he just couldn't help himself. "You're not going to that *thing* tomorrow, are you?"

Evelyn didn't turn around. "I don't know. Haven't decided."

"Please don't, honey. It'll just make you miserable."

"I'm already miserable."

"Don't you remember the last time you attended a program about the state hospital, when that artist blared Bach from the ruins of Old Main? It sent you to bed for a week."

"That was twenty years ago."

"You think this'll be different?" Donnie hugged her stiff back, the muscles rigid and unbending. "How can I help?"

"You can't." She wriggled out of his arms. "I'm going to take a walk."

"Now?" He pointed to the clock on the microwave. "It's almost nine."

She touched his cheek. "Maybe I can walk off this bad mood."

Donnie stood in the doorway, shivering in the chill night breeze. He watched Evelyn pick up a small envelope, trying to hide it from him, and shove it into her jacket pocket. He had a bad feeling about that envelope, whatever it was. He had a very bad feeling about tonight and tomorrow morning and all of it. And having his wife walking through their dark neighborhood with a who-knew-what skulking around only increased his dread.

GANDALF SIMON

Gandalf grabbed her jacket and scarf from the coat tree and called to Jess. "I'm going out to walk."

"It's cold," Jess said. "Take your warm gloves."

Gandalf wrapped a scarf around her neck and pulled on her gloves. She was grateful that Jess had stopped objecting to her nighttime walks, especially now. Their neighborhood had always been safe, probably was still safe even with the unsolved mystery of Iris's disappearance.

Gandalf loved walking alone in the dark through the quiet neighborhood that had grown up on the site of the old hospital. She could stride without thinking, up and down the half-dozen streets mostly named after former city mayors. Such an odd concept, turning a failed healing enterprise into ordinary homes. Sometimes she thought it was creepy and disrespectful. Other times it felt perfectly reasonable to recycle grief and regret into the commonplace pleasures of domestic life.

Walking past Number Five, Gandalf watched their new next-door neighbors through the open curtains. The man paced the living room, jiggling a red-faced infant in his arms. The woman stood on a stool in the kitchen area, arranging items on the top shelf of the cupboard. For the hundredth time, she wondered what would have happened if she had managed to convince Jess years ago that they should foster a child, maybe even adopt. No, life was probably better this way. Definitely simpler.

She couldn't see anything in Number Six. They always had the shades drawn tight. What did they have to hide, that odd couple with the alliterative A names?

Turning into the newer section of the neighborhood, she returned the wave of a woman walking her dachshund, spiffy in an iridescent green doggy sweater that sparkled under the streetlight, but she didn't slow down. There were a surprising number of people walking dogs at this hour. Maybe she should get a dog to keep her company on these walks and while Jess was at work. Certainly easier than a foster child.

Her nighttime walking never varied. The same streets in the same order. A consistent repeated pattern. That was the soothing nature of it. Her footsteps led her brain down the well-known sidewalks, and the motion calmed her synapses. They lulled her thoughts into a soft place where nightmares were banished, and exhaustion could often blossom unto slumber. She hummed tunelessly, not aware of any true melody, a gentle accompaniment to her footsteps. It usually took an hour for the walking to bring her to a place of calm.

Leaving the row of attached townhouses, she followed the curved driveway in front of the Haskell Building and turned right along the parking lot and loading dock. Haskell was where the last patients lived in the final years before the state hospital was closed, but it now housed state offices and agencies. It was her least favorite part of the neighborhood walk, and she always hurried past the building, ugly and solemn in its brick face and harsh lines.

Some nights, more rarely now, the bars on the Haskell windows sucked her mind back to her own incarceration, and she had to relive those four horrible days in fast forward—being kidnapped at the airport, the small plane to Hurricane Island, the interrogations, the cold and humiliation, her escape and eventual rescue. She had been touched by evil and somehow managed to survive it, but not without consequences. Those ugly nights she walked faster, expelling old ghosts with long strides and swinging arms. Those nights she walked for hours.

Lately though, she looked at the building with curiosity rather than fear. There were years after she escaped from Hurricane Island when she worried that she would end up someplace like this hospital, albeit probably a more privileged version. When she and Jess first moved to town, Gandalf read every book in the Forbes Library about the state hospital. She read about the lack of evidence-based treatments. About the women who were committed because their husbands were tired of them, the people with admitting diagnoses of masturbation or hysteria, the homosexuals locked up to protect society from their contagion.

If she'd been born a century earlier, she easily could have ended up on the other side of those barred windows.

When a shape moved on the loading dock, briefly visible against the garage door, Gandalf stopped walking. She rarely interrupted the therapeutic forward motion of her walking, but she had never seen anyone here before. The dog walkers mostly kept to the streets, maybe because the nighttime woods were home to bears and deer, foxes and skunks, ticks and poison ivy. The shadow must have seen her too because it stopped and slunk back, disappearing into the dark behind a dumpster.

Gandalf resumed walking but stopped again when she heard sobbing from the direction of the building. From the shadow on the dock? She should keep walking, or she'd never fall asleep. But when she got home and told Jess about it, Jess would ask, "How could you just walk by? Didn't you check to make sure someone wasn't hurt?"

Reluctantly, she walked toward the dock. "Hello," she called out, hoping hard that no one would answer. "Are you okay?"

AGGIE NORTH

Aggie inched the shade slightly away from the window and peeked out. That odd wizard-named woman from next door was walking again. Every fucking night she walked for hours. What was wrong with her to make her walk like that? What was wrong with this whole place?

She didn't like giving up. Once before in her life she had bailed on a place, believing that things would be better if she could only get away. She grew up in Temptation, Kentucky, a town so small it never made it to any map. A hollow so isolated you had to drive up the creek bed to get there. A town so poor the only temptations were the oblivions of sex or moonshine or home-cooked meth. She left when she finished eighth grade in the one room school, hitchhiking until her last ride, a female trucker, dropped her off at an interstate exit in Massachusetts, saying, "Try this place, sweetheart. It's paradise compared to where you came from." The trucker gave her the name of her cousin who worked for the college housekeeping department. It wasn't paradise, not for her, but she got a job and met Arnie and they did just fine.

But today was the last straw. It was bad enough living someplace where you so clearly didn't fit in. Heartbreak enough losing babies one after another, with the empty nursery down the hall mocking her every day. Scary enough having a kidnapper or worse on the loose in their neighborhood, taking that poor old woman right out of her house. But being questioned for hours by those two detectives and then dragged over to Number One, to be alibied by a child, that was the end of it. She felt humiliated and furious. Morgan was the only person she would miss if they left. If she had a daughter, she would have wanted one just like Morgan, although she would have named her something pretty. Like Chelsea or Paisley.

"I've had it," she told Arnie.

"Had what?"

"Had it with this place. This town. This street."

"Because of today? Mrs. Blum?"

"Because of everything. I want to get out of here."

"Are you sure?" Arnie asked. "This is so easy, so close to work."

"I hate it here. They hate us. I can't live like this."

"Okay," he said, kissing her forehead. "Guess it's time."

GLORIA

Gloria still had one task before calling Iris's daughter. They were parked in the Stop & Shop lot, camouflaged as ordinary grocery shoppers between an SUV and a Prius.

"I'll call your daughter from the pay phone in the store," Gloria said. "You should stay hidden under the quilts, just in case."

"Okay. Nap time."

"And, oh," Gloria said. "Could you lend me some cash?"

Iris rummaged in her purse and handed Gloria a twenty. "Get some treats," she said.

Gloria locked the car behind her. Walking up and down the store aisles with a basket, she punched a phone number on her cell and waited for her former co-worker to pick up. Roberta had been a social worker at the state hospital before joining the agency where Gloria last worked.

Roberta was surprised at Gloria's questions, but confirmed what Iris said. In the bad old days, one physician, any kind of doctor, could commit a person to the hospital. A court hearing was supposed to follow, but judges rarely questioned the doctor's assessment.

"That's horrible," Gloria said.

"Shameful," Roberta agreed. "In the late sixties they rewrote the laws, but before then, a lot of people ended up at the hospital who didn't belong there."

"And what about the staff? I know the treatments back then were pretty medieval, but were the staff kind? Did they care?"

"When? What years are you interested in?"

"Starting in the midfifties."

"I didn't start working there until much later," Roberta said. "But the first psych meds were beginning to be widely used about then. Mostly Thorazine. Patients were often pretty zonked. And yes, some of the staff were very nurturing. Some brought patients to their homes on holidays, became like family. More like family pets maybe, but still kind. Of course, there were always a few staff members who were sadistic, more ill than the patients, but they were few. They did damage though." Roberta paused before adding, "Why did you say you wanted to know about this?"

"It's complicated," Gloria said. "Let's get together soon and I'll fill you in."

Wandering up and down the aisles, Gloria looked at fancy cookies and fruit platters, at candy bars and potato chips and smoked salmon. What would a woman like Iris consider a treat? Gloria had no clue and it pained her that she didn't know. Did the daughter know what food would comfort her mother? How lucky Lexi was to have Iris for a mother.

Gloria would just have to guess. She put rosemary crackers and brie into her basket. Chocolate chip cookies and Honeycrisp apples. Then she headed to the back of the store to the pay phone to call that lucky daughter.

EVELYN TURNER

She tried to ignore the voice from the road asking, "Are you okay?"

Damn. The last thing she wanted was anyone poking around in her business. Couldn't a woman weep in peace? Crying sometimes helped. Pacing too.

If she cried at home, Donnie tried to comfort her. When he couldn't, he got sad, and she ended up needing to comfort him. She used to sit by the old stone wall next to the Coach House, the place where it happened, grinding her spine hard into the rough rocks, inviting another pain to balance the one inside. But with the Coach House renovated and students everywhere and the old stone wall now hidden behind fancy heating and cooling equipment, these days she came to Haskell.

And now there was someone out there calling to her. She scurried behind the dumpster and held her breath. Maybe the person would go away.

The voice called again. "Who's there? Do you need help?"

Double damn. It sounded like Gandalf. Of all the neighbors, she was the one Evelyn least wanted to see. She had to be the person with the lowest empathy quotient on the Court. The lucky part was that Gandalf was so stiff and uncomfortable around people, so socially inept, that she wouldn't be hard to get rid of.

Evelyn stepped out of the shadow. "It's Evelyn. Is that you, Gandalf?"

"Yes. Is something wrong?"

"I'm all right. Well, not really. I don't need anything."

Gandalf looked like she couldn't decide. Like she wanted to leave but couldn't quite do it.

"Please," Evelyn said. "Please leave."

Gandalf stepped back as if she was respecting the request, but then she stopped. "Are you sure you don't want to talk?" she asked. "You seem so sad."

Gandalf was the last person she wanted to talk to, the last person she would have expected to offer an ear on a dark and blustery November evening. But crying alone didn't ease her sadness, so maybe talking to an almost-stranger, this aloof and generally awkward neighbor, would help. Evelyn didn't understand why, after decades of shame and silence, she was now exposing her pain to anyone who would listen. It must have something to do with Iris being missing, with the reemergence of her anger at Dr. Blum, with the thick cloud of anxiety permeating Azalea Court.

"Yes," she said. "I think I would like to talk." She noted the look of surprise on Gandalf's face. It was probably mirrored on her own.

The sound of wheels on pavement struck them both at the same moment and they turned towards the road. Headlights moved slowly, then stopped and turned off.

Evelyn held a finger to her lips, then pointed to the darkness behind the dumpster. Gandalf followed her there, and they waited.

SATURDAY EVENING

What We Thought We Knew:
Cultural attitudes towards women were undoubtedly one of the factors which caused twice as many women as men to be admitted into mental institutions.

—Katherine Ellen McCarthy,
Psychiatry in the Nineteenth Century:
The Early Years of Northampton State Hospital

DETECTIVE McPHEE

Call it a gut feeling or cop radar or just a hunch. Detective McPhee switched squad assignments and gave herself the graveyard shift in the surveillance room at the downtown station. She wanted to personally examine all the camera footage, and it would give her time to think.

By ten, she was ready to admit that perhaps imagination was winning out over logic, because there was nothing going on. The Blums' neighborhood had few cameras, just at the traffic lights leading into the development, but the old state hospital building housing the state mental health agencies had several. To prevent break-ins, they said, but McPhee suspected it was in response to local teenagers' continued fascination with the old buildings, breaking in and partying in the creepy old spaces.

She scrolled through all the images since the old woman went missing, seeing nothing suspicious. Then she texted the two officers scheduled to drive through the neighborhood, part of the routine checks for a missing person.

Anything happening?

Nada

Thnx

McPhee stood up and stretched. Touched her toes. Winced. Sat down. She never did well with graveyard shift. Her wife loved working nights. She said the medical center was softer and more human in the dark. That comment always made McPhee smile; her world certainly wasn't kinder in the wee hours.

She poured a cup of coffee and returned to the cameras. Nine hours to go. To keep herself awake she mentally reviewed the residents of

Azalea Court, house by house. She was pretty certain she could cross the family in Number One off her suspect list. The gardener guy Eric with his unpleasant wife. She wondered how long that marriage would last, given the disdain in the wife's eyes when she looked at her husband. The kids seemed pretty solid though. They'd do all right.

The husband was always on top of the suspect list, and the old man was certainly hiding something, but she hadn't made up her mind about Dr. Blum. She didn't think he had done something nasty to his wife. He was probably just a typical selfish old coot, rather like her own father. Harm done over years, almost inadvertently, without malicious intent. Still, she was remiss in not bringing him in for a formal videotaped interview. Sometimes things showed up on tape that you didn't notice in person. She'd do that tomorrow.

She shook her head and finished the coffee. The couple in Number Three seemed pretty benign as well, despite the decades-old grudge the woman held and her husband's frustration with it. They most likely had nothing to do with Mrs. Blum's disappearance.

The couple in Number Four intrigued her. Once her contact at WITSEC swore there was nothing to the Witness Protection rumor, she allowed herself a short daydream about Gandalf Simon and Jess Simon. They seemed like interesting women, and McPhee and her wife didn't have many friends. Most lesbians in town didn't seem too interested in hanging out with a cop. It's not like she ever talked about cases or interrogated people at the dinner table. Gandalf and Jess were older, but maybe sometime—after the case was solved—the four of them might get together for a drink. *Don't be silly*, she told herself. *This isn't about your social life.*

Who was next? The new family with the cute baby, but they moved in after the disappearance and had no reason to want to harm Mrs. Blum. Then there was the couple in Number Six, who stuck out like a sore thumb on the Court. In the whole town, actually. The bald woman with a hoodie and her odd husband. If this were a TV cop show, he'd be the villain with his sideways glances and sly grin. But this was real life, and he was just a guy with an unfortunate face.

She would have to talk with the Blum daughter again. Lexi Blum seemed genuinely worried about her mother. And she must know things that might help, even if she didn't know she knew them. McPhee tried to concentrate on the interviews, searching her brain for the little thing someone might have said, the half-heard clue. If only she weren't so sleepy.

Did she doze off? She must have, because when she checked the wall clock again it was almost ten thirty. And the surveillance camera at the Haskell loading dock had action. A person walked slowly across the parking area towards the dumpster. Her head turned from side to side as she faced the shadows. After a moment, a second person moved out from the darkness behind the dumpster. The two people, women probably from the shape of their silhouettes, appeared to be talking. If only these cameras were wired for sound! She would have loved to hear their conversation, to know who they were and what they were doing at Haskell.

They must have heard something, because both women turned their heads sharply toward the road at the same moment. A car, maybe? The women moved together, stepping out of the light and out of view. At last, she thought. At last something is breaking with this case.

McPhee took out her phone to notify the desk sergeant that she was going to a crime scene, but then she stopped. Protocol would be to send a patrol car to check this out. But strictly speaking there was no crime. Not yet, maybe not at all.

She thought about it for a few long moments. She had to admit that she was more personally involved in this case than was smart. If one of her squad brought up this scenario, she would tell them to follow protocol and not leave her post to personally investigate. But she wanted to know what was happening. She wanted to be the one to find Iris Blum safe and sound. Against her better judgement, McPhee asked the desk sergeant to cover the surveillance room and then left the station.

LEXI BLUM

The telephone call from her mother's new friend Gloria—whoever she was, and whatever she wanted—came about ten thirty Saturday evening. Lexi had put her phone on vibrate so the call wouldn't wake her father.

"This is Lexi."

"I'm Gloria. Your mother's friend. She asked me to call."

"Is she okay?"

"She's fine. But she needs a warm place to sleep tonight."

Lexi interrupted her. "She can stay at my apartment."

"Not a good idea," Gloria said. "We don't know if the police are watching your place and my, well, my place isn't safe either."

Lexi wondered about that. If she had never heard of this Gloria friend, why would the police know about her and be keeping an eye on her house too? "What can I do? How can I help?"

"Do you have the blankets ready? And pillows, sleeping bags?"

"Yes. Two garbage bags full, in my car."

"Don't bring your car," Gloria said. "Leave it parked at your parents' house. Grab the warm stuff and plenty of hot tea and meet us at the Haskell Building. The entrance in back, near the loading dock."

"Haskell? Why?" Lexi asked.

Gloria hung up.

Lexi heated water and added tea bags. Impulsively, she rummaged in the closet for the jewelry box of things her mother never wore but couldn't bear to part with and found the locket. Lexi had loved to play with it as a child, opening and closing the minute mechanism, removing and replacing the curls. Her mother never told her whose hair was in the tarnished silver heart, just said it belonged to a dear friend from childhood. But now Lexi understood that it must be *hers*. Harriet's.

She listened at her father's bedroom door. Snores. Then she slipped out the back door of Number Two Azalea Court carrying two thermoses and a flashlight. No sign of surveillance around the circle, but that didn't mean someone wasn't watching. Keeping to the shadows at the edge of the road, she grabbed the garbage bags from her car and hurried down Prince Street to the Haskell Building. Brick, institutional, and cold, it was not a welcoming place to spend the night. Even with the industrial-sized light, the back of the building was dark and shadowy. She felt eyes on the back of her head as she walked toward the double metal doors.

Her mother and another woman stood in the shadows at the foot of the loading dock. The other woman held a yellow cat wrapped in a ratty comforter. Lexi hugged her mother hard, struggling to hold in the sobs. How long had it been since she really hugged Iris? How long since she thought of her as a mother, as a woman? Lexi had always wished that her mother had been warmer, or more involved, or more independent, or more fierce? But she had almost lost this imperfect mother and now she couldn't let her go.

"It's all right," Iris said, patting Lexi's shoulder. Iris pulled back and offered her daughter a slightly soiled hanky. Who still used handkerchiefs? Lexi dabbed her eyes and cheeks.

"This is my friend Gloria," her mother said, and Lexi turned to the other shape in the shadow. The friend looked about Lexi's own age. Gloria smiled and put her finger to her lips.

"This is Canary," she whispered, scratching the cat behind the ears.

Who was going to hear us? Lexi wondered. No one was around, although she still had the sensation of being watched. She tried to shake off the feeling. Just nerves.

"Let's get inside before someone sees us." Gloria shifted the cat in her arms and pulled a key from her pocket.

"How did you get a key?" Lexi asked.

"The hospital wasn't very careful about getting keys back from employees when they left," Gloria said. "A guy I know used to work here."

The door was heavy, opening with reluctance and creaking on rusty hinges. Once inside the dark hallway, Gloria switched on a flashlight, and Lexi did the same.

Lexi hadn't been inside since the state hospital was closed, over a quarter-century earlier. They were on the first floor, in the wing where the "female elderly chronics" were once housed. The old chest-high half walls now extended to the ceiling, blocking their view into those rooms, but Lexi remembered them clearly from her unauthorized visits as a child and teenager. The walls were tiled, easy to hose down the bodily fluids that seeped or spewed from miserable women with no privacy and no power. Lexi grabbed her mother's hand, glad that Iris couldn't see through the walls into those rooms, just like the one where her friend Harriet might have been kept.

"Where are we going?" Lexi asked.

"The basement," Gloria said.

"The basement?" Iris asked. "That's where the tunnel entrance is. Horrible places. I think they're all blocked off now."

Gloria nodded. "They are. But there's a room down there where we can sleep. My friend with the key brought me here one night last winter when it was really cold. It's not nice, but it's warmer than outside. He swore he'd never come back because he saw ghosts in the tunnel. He decided that a warm and dry place to sleep isn't worth ghosts stealing your breath while you sleep. Or whatever they do. He passed the key on to me and warned me to watch out for the night guard." Gloria shined her flashlight on her watch. "We'll have to be quiet and keep the lights off. The guard comes through here every few hours and I don't know the schedule. I've thought about sleeping here, but never have."

Iris squeezed Lexi's hand. "Gloria lost her home. She lives in her car. With her cat. And she rescued me."

Lexi stared at the homeless woman. Then she took a deep breath and smiled wanly. "Thanks for helping my mom. I know this basement a bit too. Kids in the neighborhood broke in here all the time. This was our local haunted house."

"You did that?" Iris asked.

"Great place to smoke weed and have sex. Not me, of course." She glanced at Iris. "Until some of my friends got lost one night and ended up in the hallway to the morgue. They found jars with parts of brains in formaldehyde."

Iris covered her mouth with her hand. She knew that Lexi liked to sneak out at night. Harmless fun, she had thought, but brains in jars were nasty.

Lexi shined her flashlight on the entrance to a stairwell. "Those go downstairs."

Iris took the stairs slowly, using her cane and holding Lexi's arm. The thick mustiness of the air in the basement made it hard to breathe. Or maybe it wasn't the damp. Maybe it was the crowding of ghosts, even though she didn't believe in them. Could they really steal breath from the living?

"That corridor leads to the tunnel," Lexi said, pointing the light to the left.

Iris nodded. "When Asher worked here, I sometimes walked with him through the tunnels from one building to another. I wonder if . . ." Her voice faded into silence.

"I know about Harriet, Mom," Lexi said. "I know what Dad did."

"I can't talk about all that now, dear." Her mother squeezed her eyes closed. "But I do wonder if Harriet ever stood right here. In this very spot where we're standing."

"It's possible, I guess," Lexi said.

Iris turned to Gloria. "I need to see the tunnel entrance. Just for a minute."

The hallway to the tunnel sloped downward and the air became thicker, fouler. Water filled the tunnel almost to the entry. The musty smell was harsh and raw, making the women clear their throats every few seconds.

Iris stifled a gag. All that rain. She took Lexi's hand and shined the light on the tunnel wall ahead, mottled with mold and who knows what else. Ameboid shapes, large and free form, flowed from concrete floor to ceiling in shades of grays and greens.

The cat growled.

"I suppose those could be the ghosts my friend saw," Gloria said. "Canary senses something here and he's smart."

"The ghosts might be real." Iris pointed to the person-shaped figure on the left. "Look. That could be Harriet. Something about the stoop of her shoulders and all that hair." She leaned forward to study the shapes. "I want to feel Harriet's presence here."

Iris felt the worried gaze of her daughter and her friend, but this was no time to back down. It had taken her decades to find Harriet and she couldn't stop now. "See. She's standing close to another shape. Maybe Harriet had a friend." Iris staggered slightly with the rush of her feelings. Lexi tightened her grip on Iris's arm.

"Rebecca," Gloria offered. "That other shape could be her friend Rebecca. You know, from Rebecca's Way?"

Iris smiled, then shook her head, trying to find some inner balance, some control over her wild imaginings. "What am I saying? There's no such thing as ghosts. Maybe your father is right about me losing my mind."

"Don't go there, Mom. His pills made you confused. Your mind is fine."

Iris closed her eyes and swayed again, then regained her balance by leaning against an old wood-slatted laundry cart on rusty wheels. She imagined Harriet hiding in the cart, burrowed under dingy sheets and towels, easily big enough for a woman trying to hide. She wondered if Harriet ever had tried to escape. The Harriet she knew would have tried to get free, even if she had been doped up and restrained and locked away. Did people ever manage to break out of this place? How horrible was it, day to day? How did the hospital staff treat people like Harriet?

Her daughter read her mind. "Do you think the people who worked here, who worked for Dad, were kind to Harriet?" Lexi asked.

"I hope so," Iris said, but she didn't know. She knew the reputation state mental institutions had and all the stories she had heard from Asher over decades. It was possible that the attendants and nurses had been sympathetic and gentle with her dear Harriet.

"Harriet is one of my lost women," Lexi said.

"Who are they?" Gloria asked.

"The women who didn't belong here. Whose husbands or fathers used this place as a garbage can," Lexi said. "I collect their stories."

How odd about those women! Her husband had a major role in locking them up and her daughter wanted to collect them. What did *they* want? Their accusatory voices bounced and echoed in the tunnel entrance, a thick and constant murmur, an imagined chorus of unhappy souls. Come on, Iris told herself. It's just an old tunnel, flooded and musty and gross. There's no such thing as ghosts.

Gloria's voice interrupted her musings. "Let's go back. I'm worried about the guard. The storage room has a little heat. We can sleep there."

Sleep? How could they possibly sleep in that awful place?

ASHER BLUM

Asher couldn't sleep. He hadn't slept more than two hours at a time since Iris left. Was that only yesterday? How could that be? Perhaps he would never sleep again. He considered staying in bed, but if he was awake, he might as well do some work. He struggled into his bathrobe and opened his bedroom door. The house was dark and quiet. It was quiet in the guest bedroom; Lexi must be able to sleep. He tiptoed past her door into the living room for a glass of water. A small envelope, the size that might hold a sympathy card or thank you note, had been shoved through the mail slot and stared at him from the floor.

Not a greeting card, nor a thank you note. A single piece of lined paper, ripped from a notebook, with only three short sentences: *Thirty-five years ago, a doctor raped me at your precious hospital. You did nothing. You deserve all the pain I hope you're feeling today.*

His eyes closed. His body slumped against the wall. He felt the weight of his ninety-four years. The decades were boulders on his shoulders, sharp burrs under his pajamas, fire ants crawling up his bare ankles. He had made so many mistakes.

The note must have come from his next-door neighbor, Evelyn. He knew that she hated him, and he remembered the incident. The doctor who assaulted her was young and stupid and probably deserved to have his residency ended. It wasn't actually Asher's call; the medical education director made the decision not to destroy the guy's career. There was outcry from some staff, but Asher felt sorry for the young doctor and let the decision stand. The hospital was already under public scrutiny. The overcrowding was severe, funding was terribly inadequate, the consent decree had been established, and the closing of the hospital was already in the works. What good would firing one psychiatrist-in-training do? He remembered asking his best social worker, Roberta Somebody, to help Evelyn. Then he had put the incident out of his mind.

Clearly a mistake. One of many, apparently. But this note made him uncomfortable. He felt threatened. Evelyn had a reputation for being quick tempered and mean, in addition to not minding her own business. Could she somehow be involved in Iris's disappearance? Should he call that detective and let her know?

No, that was being paranoid. He tucked the angry words deep into Iris's knitting basket and walked to the back door. Standing in the open doorway, he wrapped his bathrobe tighter and looked into the chilly dark of his yard. Next door, the blue spruce Eric's children planted one Christmas was haloed by a streetlight. The tangy smell of evergreen always sent him reeling back to the forest, back to his sister and the yelling of the soldiers who found her. She was gone—his sister and his parents and brother. Everyone gone.

Now his Iris was gone too. He was alone and all the things he had done to protect himself and his family were ganging up on him. Were those actions wrong? Was he wrong? Had he made the wrong choices?

How was a man supposed to know these things?

DONNIE TURNER

Donnie paced. Evelyn had been gone for over two hours and he was getting worried. This wasn't like her. The whole past month wasn't like her. Obsessing about that memorial park program tomorrow morning for one thing. And now she was describing the rape to anyone who would listen, after refusing to talk about it at all for decades.

He had tried to be supportive. Tried to get her help, all those years ago. But Evelyn was adamant. He suggested a therapist, but she wanted no part of that. He told her stories about the old hospital, the way it was when he was growing up. But when he described the satisfaction his mother felt working there, Evelyn reminded him that a patient had stabbed his mother in the arm with a pair of sewing scissors. He talked about the two old men, chronic patients, who shared Thanksgiving at their home every year. Uncle Micky and Uncle Charles, he was supposed to call them. His mother wept when Charles died, but she continued inviting Micky every year until she passed. Evelyn told him she had been terrified of Uncle Micky the first time he came to Thanksgiving, the way the old guy gobbled his food and wiped his mouth on his shirt sleeve.

All this wallowing in the past was driving him crazy. He couldn't stand it any longer. He found the leaflet Evelyn had made. The detective had written her cell phone number at the bottom for all the Azalea Court residents. He punched in the number.

"McPhee," the detective answered.

"Evelyn is missing," Donnie blurted. "She left the house hours ago. Said she was going for a walk, but she's *never* gone this long." He paused. "Oh. This is Donnie Turner, Evelyn's husband?"

"Try to relax, sir," McPhee said. "We're patrolling the neighborhood."

"This isn't like her and with Iris disappearing, I'm worried Evie is in trouble too."

"I'll let the patrol cars know to look out for her," McPhee promised, "and I'll head over there and take a look. Please, you need to stay at home, in case she returns and needs help."

Reluctantly, he agreed.

EVELYN TURNER

From their hiding spot behind the dumpster, Evelyn and Gandalf watched the two women as they walked from the car to the loading dock door.

"That's Iris," Evelyn said, beginning to stand. "She looks all right!"

Gandalf put one finger to her lips, and restrained Evelyn with the other hand. "Wait," she whispered.

Evelyn nodded. "Who's the woman with the cat?" She looked vaguely familiar, but Evelyn couldn't identify her in the poor light. They stood at the door watching the street. Within a few minutes, a third woman joined them.

"That's Lexi," Evelyn said, relaxing her tight shoulders.

The metal door creaked open and the three women entered the dark building. As the door started to close, Evelyn knew what she had to do. Quietly, she grabbed a broken two-by-four sticking out of the dumpster and slipped it into the doorway, preventing the door from closing completely. Then she returned to the shadows.

"Why did you do that?" Gandalf asked.

"I don't know who that is with Iris and Lexi. I want to make sure Iris is really safe."

"She's with her daughter. Why wouldn't she be safe? Who brings a cat when committing a felony? Besides, do you think the daughter kidnapped her own mother?"

"You think people never harm the ones closest to them?" Evelyn said. "In my work you see all sorts of awful things done by the nearest and dearest." She hesitated. "Besides, I'm nosy. I'm sure you've heard that about me. I want to know what's going on."

"So, what are you waiting for?"

"Let's give them some time to get wherever they're going. Then we'll go in."

Gandalf shook her head. "I'm not sure I want to get involved."

"You *are* involved. You offered your help when I needed you. Let's see this through together."

"I don't know. Breaking into a deserted hospital is not the same as listening to a person."

"True, but we have to help Iris." She touched Gandalf's hand. "You helped me already. By not just walking by. Thank you."

Gandalf didn't pull her hand away.

"Oh, what the hell. I'm no damn good at waiting," Evelyn said. "Let's go in."

They opened the door just enough to slip inside, hoping the three women were already far enough away to not hear the screech. As it closed, Gandalf returned the board back into the doorway to prevent it closing.

"Why did you do that?" Evelyn asked.

"So we can get out."

"These kinds of doors open from the inside."

"This was a mental hospital," Gandalf said. "People were locked up in here and they couldn't escape. I want to be certain we can get out."

"Makes sense." Evelyn turned on her phone flashlight, and they started walking down the hallway.

"I was locked up once." Gandalf spoke into the dark. "It was a civilian detention center in Maine, and I was held prisoner. I couldn't stand to be confined like that again. Ever."

"For real?" Evelyn shined the flashlight at Gandalf's face. "What did you do?"

GANDALF SIMON

"Nothing! I did nothing," Gandalf whispered, pushing away the bright light. Why had she thought this busybody woman would understand, would offer any kind of comfort? "Never mind. Where are we going?"

"I'm sorry," Evelyn said. "That comment was unkind. I have a big mouth. Please, tell me what happened to you."

Gandalf shook her head and started walking away from someone else who didn't understand. Then she stopped herself. If there was ever a person to share her story with, Evelyn might be that person. Someone odd, like her, and seeming apart from others. "I was kidnapped by Homeland Security and held captive. Tortured, though they called it enhanced interrogation. It broke me."

Evelyn stared at her, mouth open. She grabbed Gandalf's arm.

"I'll tell you the story another time. Now, please let us find Iris and get out of here. This place gives me the creeps."

It did. It seriously creeped her out. Something about institutional hallways with closed doors at regular intervals. These floors were tiled rather than wooden like the detention center in Maine, but the walls held the same silenced voices, the same dank odor of broken lives and hopeless yearning.

Gandalf kept walking, sensing Evelyn following her, until she reached the darker cavern of a stairwell. Gandalf was thrust back in time, facing a similar darkness in Maine. Back then, she hugged the institutional hallway with a hurricane roaring outside, her life depending on her ability to escape. She wasn't sure she could do this now, relive that moment this way. She should turn back. But what if Evelyn was right? What if the old woman needed rescuing? What if Iris's life depended on them?

"Listen," Evelyn said. A brief murmur of voices drifted up from the floor below. "Sounds like they're downstairs."

At the bottom of the stairs they saw a strip of light under a doorway to the left and walked quietly in that direction. Gandalf tried not to look too closely at the patterns of mold blooming on the wall, not to breathe too deeply the ancient musty air.

"Should we just go in?" Gandalf asked.

"I don't know. What if they're holding Iris against her will? Maybe one of us should stay out here, so we can go for help?"

"I'll stay," Gandalf offered, but then the door opened to Lexi holding a broom like a baseball bat. When she saw Evelyn and Gandalf, Lexi lowered the broom. Gandalf tried to relax, but every muscle fiber was engaged. She couldn't stay in the hallway, even to stand guard, and stepped forward to join Evelyn at the door. No way could she stay behind by herself in the cold hallway, both empty and crowded with some kind of presence.

"I'm glad it's you," Lexi said. "But what are you doing here?"

"Gandalf and I were out walking," Evelyn said. "We saw you with Iris and wanted to help. Is she okay? What is this room?"

This room, Gandalf thought, is in an abandoned mental institution with the ghosts of crazy people all locked up in the dead of night. She must be nuts to be here. And Jess, she must be wild with worry by now.

The third woman joined Lexi. "This is a storeroom for the old hospital. And you'd better come in. There's a night guard who patrols this building."

"Quiet." Lexi put her finger to her lips. "My mom is trying to sleep."

She stepped back to let them enter the room, crowded with stacks of sagging cardboard boxes, piles of rusty box springs, unidentifiable equipment covered in dust. Mismatched chairs in a makeshift circle were heaped with blankets and pillows and sleeping bags; opened packages of cookies and chips and thermoses covered an upturned carton.

Iris slept on her side on an old sofa, covered by a faded comforter and sleeping bag. The yellow cat was curled against her chest. Lexi sat down at her mother's feet, and the other women took chairs around the circle.

"What's going on?" Evelyn asked.

"My mother asked Gloria for help," Lexi said. "And Gloria called me."

"I don't understand," Evelyn said. "Why did Iris go missing and what's going on?"

"It's a long story," Lexi said. "Come get comfortable and we'll talk. If you are here to help my mother, that is."

Evelyn and Gandalf both nodded. Yes. Of course.

Gandalf looked around and realized she felt relaxed and strangely calm in this extraordinary situation. What was wrong with her, to be more comfortable in this chaos than in ordinary life?

"Who are you?" Evelyn interrupted, pointing to Gloria. "Why do you look so familiar?"

GLORIA

"I look familiar because you stopped by my car yesterday and gave me a flyer about Iris being missing," Gloria said.

"Oh, you're the homeless woman with the blue station wagon, right?" Evelyn asked.

Lexi's glance was sharp, and Gloria recognized her reaction, somewhere between fear and blame. No time to worry about that now.

Gloria nodded. "Iris knocked on my window not long after you came by. She asked me for help. She said she was running away from her husband. But who are you?" Gloria looked at Gandalf.

"I live at Number Four," Gandalf said. "I'm not really involved in this, I guess. I barely know any of you."

Evelyn leaned over to touch Gandalf's shoulder. "Stop saying that. You *are* involved." She turned back to Lexi. "I don't understand. Why was your mother running away? I have no use for your father. Actually, I hate the man. But what did he do to Iris?"

Lexi and Gloria started telling the story. Iris woke up and joined them, the three women interrupting each other, leapfrogging over years of secrets and lies, accusations and questions. Lexi sat close to Iris. Evelyn and Gandalf listened, heads turning back and forth between the storytellers. When they were finished, Evelyn stood up.

"I'm furious at Asher," she announced. "I mean, even more than before. Let's teach the bastard a lesson. Let's kidnap him, feed him all those nasty meds he gave Iris, and keep him captive for a while."

Gandalf visibly paled. Gloria shook her head. "That might kill him."

"He essentially killed Harriet. So that would be fair," Evelyn said.

"We could hold a citizen's court. You know, make him admit his crimes. And I've got another crime to add to the indictment."

"Evelyn, remember you're talking about my father," Lexi said, her voice quivering.

Iris rubbed her eyes. "He did very bad things, but he doesn't deserve being kidnapped or drugged. Or killed."

"I suppose that Harriet might disagree with that, if she could speak for herself," Gloria said.

"And Harriet's daughter," Lexi added. "She might want some justice too."

"What daughter?" Iris asked.

"What daughter?" Evelyn, Gandalf, and Gloria repeated in unison.

"What daughter?" Iris asked again. "Please, Lexi. How on earth could Harriet have a daughter?"

How do you tell your elderly mother that her dead friend gave birth to, and then lost, a daughter? Lexi sat close to Iris on the sofa and put both arms around her mother's frail body.

"I made Dad tell me everything," Lexi said. "How he had Harriet fired, and that led to her being called before that subcommittee. How Harriet showed up at the hospital threatening him and he had her committed. How he kept her quiet with psych meds. How she tried to kill herself and eventually succeeded."

"I know all that, dear," Iris interrupted. "What about the daughter?"

"Two years after Harriet was locked up in the hospital, she got pregnant. Dad couldn't find out if she was raped or had consensual sex."

"How could she consent if she was imprisoned, drugged?" Gloria asked.

"Just because a person is incarcerated doesn't mean they can't still have the full range of human emotions," Gandalf said quietly.

Lexi looked at Gandalf. What did she mean by that? Was she talking about consent, or something else?

"It was probably rape," Evelyn blurted. "I was raped at that hospital just a few years later. It was a horrible place!"

Gandalf scooted her chair closer to Evelyn and took her hand.

There didn't seem to be any way to further respond to Evelyn, so Lexi continued. "Dad made sure Harriet had good prenatal care, decreased her meds to protect the baby during the pregnancy. The baby was born, a girl, and they took her away."

Iris cried out. "Oh, poor Harriet! I wonder if she ever got to see her baby, hold her. Do you suppose she understood what was happening, or was she so doped up she didn't know?"

Lexi squeezed her mother's shoulders. "I don't know. Probably, Harriet never saw the baby. Dad arranged for her to be adopted."

"When was the baby born?" Iris asked.

"September 1958."

Gloria made a strangled sound in her throat, as if she started to speak and cut herself off.

Iris looked at her. "Are you all right, dear?"

Gloria nodded and stroked Canary.

"Dad wasn't sure of the exact date," Lexi continued. "She was adopted by a local family. He kept track of the girl for years, until she went to college. He tried to access the adoption papers a few years ago but was told they were destroyed in a fire. He says that's all he knows."

Iris was silent, then asked. "Do you know her name?"

"No. No other details, Mom. I'm sorry."

A gust of wind rattled the old basement windows and the women sat quietly, listening.

"I've been thinking about ghosts," Evelyn said. "The new woman in Number Five believes that our ancestors, our community elders, stick around to watch over us. Maybe all the people, all the women, who lived and died here are still around. Maybe they're in this room with us. I can almost feel their presence."

"Like Harriet and Rebecca," Gloria said.

The cat growled, deep in his throat.

"See, Canary agrees with me," Gloria said.

Before Lexi could answer, the door to the hallway opened.

DETECTIVE McPHEE

By the time McPhee got to Haskell, there was no sign of anyone at the loading dock. Where were the two women she'd seen on the surveillance images and how did they get inside? She parked her car and examined the area with her flashlight. Nothing behind the dumpster, but the pattern of footsteps in the unswept leaves on the dock suggested more than two people.

Then she noticed a board stuck into the doorway. She again considered calling the station for backup. She *should* do that. It was absolutely the prudent thing to do, not to mention the protocol that could keep her out of trouble if things went south. But she had seen too many situations get out of hand when police officers went barging in with weapons drawn. Stress and fear and darkness could make people react with more force than thought. And when people with guns—even well-trained cops with guns—get involved, people sometimes get hurt. Her gut told her this was probably a situation requiring conversation, perhaps mediation, rather than armed cops. Still, she unzipped her jacket and released the safety strap on her holster. Just in case.

Inside the heavy door, she replaced the board. As a public servant she probably should secure the building, but they might need backup after all, or even emergency medical services, and a locked metal door would significantly slow down any responders. She stood in the dark hallway and listened for voices. Nothing. Shining her flashlight on the floor, she followed scuff marks in the dust along the corridor and down one flight of stairs. There was a strip of light under a doorway to the left, and soft voices.

She stood at the door and listened. The voices were muffled, and she couldn't hear clearly enough to recognize anyone. The conversation sounded ordinary, friendly even. Still, she placed her hand lightly on her firearm, opened the door and entered.

The room was large, with stacked boxes, old file cabinets, dusty equipment. On a sagging plaid sofa, an old woman with flyaway white hair stared at her, fear on her face and a cat on her lap. Lexi sat next to the old woman. Gandalf from Number Four and Evelyn from Number Three stared also. Another woman too, someone she hadn't met before.

McPhee stepped into the circle and squatted down in front of the elderly woman. "I'm Detective McPhee. Are you Iris Blum? Are you all right?"

Iris nodded. "Yes, and yes. I'm fine, dear. Sorry to cause so much trouble."

McPhee stood up and looked around the circle. "Okay, ladies. What's going on here? Mrs. Blum, would you please fill me in on what happened to you?"

Iris answered for them all. "I will try to fully answer all your questions, Detective. But please, humor an old woman for a moment. My daughter just said something very surprising and then the ghosts came, and my head is spinning trying to understand it all." She closed her eyes and leaned against her daughter.

Ghosts? What was going on with these women?

LATE SATURDAY NIGHT

What We Thought We Knew:
Many women in asylums were not insane; 'help' was not to be found in doctor-headed, attendant-staffed, and state-run patriarchal institutions, neither in the nineteenth century nor in the twentieth.

—Phyllis Chesler,
Foreword, *Women of the Asylum: Voices from Behind the Walls*

THE WOMEN

If you had asked us what we felt as we sat around the lopsided circle in the chill of that dusty, murky room, we probably couldn't have put words to the feelings. Maybe we would have murmured something about how unexpected friendships were forged in times of trouble. Something about how dire circumstances can both tear people apart and bind them together. Something about seeing how trauma has affected someone else might loosen something stuck and rigid in ourselves.

We might have also mentioned that although none of us believed in ghosts, not really, we were beginning to suspect that when you scratch the surface of a place with so much history and such deep power, unexplained and possibly uncanny things can slip up through the cracks.

Perhaps we wouldn't have told you this for fear of your ridicule or your condemnation, but we felt the presence of Harriet and Rebecca and the other lost women Lexi collected joining us in our circle. They didn't say anything, and never really came into clear focus, but we all knew they were there. And they were joyful to be welcomed.

LEXI BLUM

Lexi followed McPhee's suspicious gaze as it traveled from woman to woman around the huddled circle. Ever since Iris mentioned ghosts, the detective seemed even more dubious. How could they explain why Iris left Azalea Court? How do you condense six-plus decades of a man's deception and lies into a concise incident report of a marriage gone wrong? How do you find the courage to unravel together the final layer, his last lie of omission to his wife?

The women were all quiet for a few minutes. Then McPhee repeated her question. "Mrs. Blum. I need to know your status. Did anyone harm or threaten you? Were you afraid to stay in your home?"

Leaning against Lexi's shoulder, Iris told the whole miserable story again, from Harriet's political activities in Brooklyn, and the awful things Asher did, to her precipitous decision to leave home the day before. McPhee started taking notes but gave up, looking overwhelmed by the barely interlocking pieces of the story. They all felt dazed, for that matter.

Iris looked at Gloria. "You look stunned, dear. Is something wrong?"

Gloria shook her head.

"I have two questions, Mom," Lexi said. "First, what made you search Dad's papers back in October, when you discovered that Harriet had been at the hospital?"

"You know what a mess his office is and how he hates me to clean in there? But once every month or two I go in anyway, just to dust and vacuum. That day, he had left his desk file drawer open and I spotted a folder with Harriet's name. It just jumped up at me. So, of course, I picked up the file and read it."

For a moment, Lexi felt sorry for her father, for his bad luck. But just for a moment. "And then, once you knew about it, once you confronted him with your knowledge, why did you wait a month before leaving, without planning where you would go or what you would do? What happened to make you leave yesterday?"

"I thought about it the whole month, night and day. And my brain wasn't working right on Asher's drugs, so it was hard to think clearly. I didn't know what to do, how to make things right. There's no way to make it right." Iris started to cry. Canary licked her hand.

"But why yesterday?" McPhee asked. "Did something else happen?"

"Yesterday was Harriet's birthday." Iris buried her face in her hands.

Lexi remembered the locket. She pulled it from her pocket and held it out to her mother. "This is from Harriet, isn't it?"

Iris pressed the locket to her lips. "She gave it to me at my wedding. To always remember her." She leaned close to Gloria and whispered, "You've been so quiet. Are you sure nothing is bothering you?"

Gloria took Iris's hand and spoke quietly so that only Iris and Lexi could hear. "Not bothering me, exactly. Just that I was born in September 1958. And I was adopted. I don't know who my birth mother was. My adopted parents always called her 'that poor unfortunate soul,' but they wouldn't tell me anything else." Gloria looked at Iris, emotion written in hard sorrow on her face. "I know it sounds crazy, and it probably doesn't make *any* logical sense, but could I possibly be your friend's daughter?"

Lexi stared at Gloria. Was this possible? Might she have to share her mother with this stranger? This homeless woman?

The cat growled deep in her throat. Louder than usual, interrupted by a door banging open and an angry shout.

"Hands up! All of you." An older man in a guard uniform stood framed in the doorway, pistol pointed at them, his hand visibly shaking. "What's going on?"

"Damn," Gloria said. "The lights. We forgot to turn off the lights."

The guard pointed his gun at each of the women in turn. "Who are you people? You shouldn't be in here. You are trespassing. Breaking the law!"

IRIS BLUM

Iris wasn't sure she could take any more surprise entrances to this chilly dusty room. Not that she had much choice.

"Stand down, sir," McPhee said. She showed him her badge and ID. "I'm Police Detective McPhee. This is an official investigation. Everything is under control."

The guard frowned, looking like he didn't believe Detective McPhee, but he lowered his gun. "You're trespassing," he repeated. He took photos of her badge and identification, then wrote down the names of the women in his pocket notebook. Iris gave him her maiden name, not ready to be officially found.

"You shouldn't be here, any of you. Don't care who you are," the guard blustered. "I want you all out. You've got ten minutes before I call 911." He jabbed his finger in McPhee's direction. "I know the police chief, and I'm going to report this, you can bet on that."

After he left the room, McPhee faced the women. Iris could tell that the detective was trying to soften her expression, but it remained stone-faced and harsh. She must be scared, Iris thought. The detective had been so kind, but her bosses probably wouldn't see it that way. They might think she had really messed up, not reporting that a missing person was found, letting them all stay here and talk. No doubt there was some protocol she should have followed, sending them home, and reporting back to the precinct. A protocol the detective had purposely ignored, at her own peril. For them. For her.

McPhee frowned. She turned from Iris to Lexi to Evelyn to Gandalf to Gloria, then back to Iris. "I have to report to headquarters that you are safe, Mrs. Blum. Right away. I should call the paramedics and have them take you to the hospital to be checked out. I must also tell the newspaper to cut the story scheduled for tomorrow morning, asking people to look for you. And we've got to get out of here," she added. "You do all understand that we're guilty of trespassing on state property. There could be charges."

"Can't you wait and call in tomorrow?" Lexi asked. "We need tonight just for ourselves please."

"Absolutely," Evelyn said, leaning forward in her chair. "We need to plan something dramatic tomorrow, at the Garden Memorial. Personally, I still think we should kidnap Dr. Blum and publicly torture him."

McPhee held up her hand. "Whoa!"

Evelyn sank back in her seat.

"Torture?" Iris shook her head. "Please, no."

"If we can't punish Dr. Blum," Evelyn insisted, "we can still destroy his reputation. We can shame him."

McPhee interrupted them. "You can discuss this later, but we can't stay here. You heard what the guard said. We all must leave now. Your families are probably all terrified, afraid that you've disappeared just like Mrs. Blum. No doubt they've all been calling 911. That's what your husband did, Evelyn. He reported that the Azalea Court kidnapper struck again. Why don't you all go home and reassure your loved ones? Then you can get together first thing in the morning and plan the Memorial."

"Instead, what if we all go to my house," Gandalf said, looking surprised at her invitation. "We can stay together. It's warmer than this place. We can plan for tomorrow and then get some sleep."

"Fine," McPhee said. "But first, everyone call home." She turned to Lexi.

"Ms. Blum, you must call your father; he's probably insane with worry. No irony intended. Evelyn and Gandalf, please call home right now." She waved her arm at the women and they both walked away from the group to make their calls.

Lexi looked at her mother. "Shall I call Dad?" she whispered.

"Let him suffer a few more hours," Iris whispered back. "Serves him right."

McPhee pulled her chair closer to Iris. She wrapped the comforter snug around the old woman's shoulders.

"Are you sure you feel okay? No trouble breathing? No dizziness or pain or heart palpitations? I wish you'd let me take you to the hospital to be checked out."

"I feel fine, and I don't want to go to the hospital. Lexi will keep an eye on me, in case anything changes. You've done your duty, dear, and I refuse."

"We'll do the necessary paperwork in the morning," McPhee said. "But I'm going to report in now so that the desk sergeant can stop the newspaper story. The press may still come to your house asking questions, Mrs. Blum. I can't help that."

"Fine," Iris said. "They'll go to my house, and I won't be there. They can bother Asher with their questions." She smiled to herself. Asher disliked being challenged and especially hated not knowing what was going on.

McPhee swiped at her phone and walked away to make her call as Gandalf returned to the center of the room.

"Jess is on her way to pick us up," Gandalf said. She started folding blankets and stacking pillows. "She will heat up some soup and make up the sofa bed. Since she is the MC for the memorial program tomorrow morning, she'll help us plan our . . . whatever it is."

Evelyn rejoined the group and began gathering their coats and scarves. "Donnie isn't happy about it, but he won't say anything about Iris being found. Let's get out of here."

McPhee returned to the group, looking pale and confused.

"You look exhausted, Detective," Lexi said. "Thank you for everything. You are welcome to join us at Gandalf's house. We'll be safe there, and from now on, my mother will be our responsibility, my responsibility. But you don't have to babysit us anymore. We won't be trespassing, and you can get to your reports."

"It's a little late for that," McPhee said. "The Haskell guard called the station to report me. My supervisor is furious. I've been suspended."

EVELYN TURNER

Azalea Court was silent in the wee hours. The women tried to be quiet as they left the cars and traipsed into Number Four. Maybe it was the headlights, or a car door closing, or their voices reminding each other about pillows and blankets and don't forget the cat. Evelyn noticed the porch light go on in Number Five and pointed it out to the others. Almost immediately, a tall woman opened the door, wrapped in a thick bathrobe.

"Is everything okay out here?" she called. Then she touched her chest. "I'm Winda and I just moved in today. I couldn't sleep and heard you. Are you all right?"

Evelyn waved the other women into the house and walked to Winda's front yard. "We're fine," she said. "I'm Evelyn and I met your husband and daughter earlier today. Or yesterday, I guess. I live over there." She gestured to Number Three. "Everything's okay. And this isn't typical Azalea Court behavior. Really."

Winda looked dubious but nodded. "Okay," she said. "I heard that a neighbor was missing, so I wanted to make sure, you know, that everyone is all right."

"I'll explain it all later," Evelyn promised. She wanted to add something about ghosts, to ask Winda all the questions crowding her mind, but for once she decided not to talk out of turn. "Thanks for checking on us."

In Gandalf's living room, Evelyn told the women about their neighbor's concern while Jess served bowls of chicken soup.

"I'm glad it wasn't someone else who heard us," Evelyn said. "She seemed cool with it."

She looked at the women settled around Jess and Gandalf's living room. Iris sat between Lexi and Gloria on the sofa, Gandalf in the recliner, Jess, McPhee, and herself on dining room chairs brought in to complete the circle. The only sounds were the sipping of soup, the clink of spoons on ceramic bowls. Their eyelids grew relaxed and heavy.

"Wait," Evelyn said. "Before we all fall asleep, can we talk about the Memorial Program?"

"We might have to get some rest first," Gandalf said, collecting empty bowls. "Could we figure it out in the morning. *Later* in the morning?"

Lexi dug in her bag for her laptop. "You guys can sleep, but I need to look again at the old hospital reports. I've been studying them for years, trying to gather data about my lost women, but I've never seen anything about patients being pregnant. I'm going to search for that."

"I don't need to be here for that," McPhee said. "Now that you're safe, I'm going home to my wife and my bed."

"I'm so sorry you got in trouble for helping us," Lexi said. "Can we help?"

McPhee shrugged. "I broke the rules. Ignored protocol."

"What happens next?" Lexi asked.

"There'll be an investigation, and there's a grievance process. But in the meantime, I'm suspended." She frowned. "I'm pretty screwed. My supervisor doesn't respect female cops, so I'm not that optimistic. But I'll let you know how it turns out."

"Before you go," Iris said, "I want you to be with us to hear our news. Gloria's and my news." She patted Gloria's hand. "It's hard to take in. I can't believe my good fortune. But I believe that Gloria is Harriet's daughter."

There was silence and then an explosion of voices. Gandalf raised her eyebrows and exchanged glances with McPhee, then shrugged and joined in the congratulations. Evelyn noticed the shadow crossing Lexi's face and then its disappearance. Iris seemed almost giddy with pleasure. Evelyn thought about her son, and when was the last time she had visited him in Brooklyn, and why didn't she go more often? She would call this afternoon, after the memorial program.

Gloria shook her head, stunned. "It seems so farfetched, but it *could* be true. Or maybe I just want it to be true. To be connected to you all."

"We could try to find out for sure," McPhee said. "Do you have anything of Harriet's that might contain DNA? I could take samples to the lab for analysis."

"But you're suspended," Gandalf said.

"The lab won't know that," McPhee said. "At least not immediately."

"The locket, Mom," Lexi said. "Doesn't hair have DNA?"

Iris shook her head. "Thank you, Detective, but we don't need DNA."

"Don't you want to know for sure?" Evelyn asked.

"Facts aren't the whole truth." Iris put the locket around Gloria's neck and kissed her cheek, then turned to face the other women. "I'm not gaga yet. I know that Gloria is probably not actually Harriet's missing daughter. But Gloria took me in when I needed help. So, I choose Gloria as Harriet's girl, and that makes her my adopted daughter too. And your sister, Lexi. I don't need DNA. My heart tells me this is right."

LEXI BLUM

Lexi hunched over her laptop in the darkened living room, frustrated that the annual hospital reports did not yield the information she wanted. At Evelyn's urging, she had added rape to the list of search words, along with pregnancy, childbirth, infant, abortion, and adoption.

"Listen to this." Lexi looked up from her laptop, but only Evelyn was awake. "This first mention of reproductive issues at all is in 1940. They report that one woman died that year from 'Diseases of Pregnancy, Childbirth and the Puerperal State.'"

"What happened to her?" Evelyn asked.

"That's all. No explanation. The year before, the pathologist reported that seven pregnancy tests were performed, with no information about the results or why the tests were ordered. This is nuts. They report the weights in precise pounds of each crop grown in the hospital gardens, but nothing about female patients being pregnant or giving birth? How can they think that 4,008 pounds of cauliflower and 85,324 pounds of potatoes are more important than the health and wellness of the women in their care?"

"Hmmmm," murmured Evelyn.

Lexi closed the laptop, careful not to jostle her mother, and considered the women dozing in Jess and Gandalf's living room. Iris sat to Lexi's right, mother's head resting on daughter's shoulder. Probably physically closer than they'd been in years. Gloria sat on Iris's other side, with the yellow cat sprawled half on Iris's lap, half on Gloria's. First known to them as the homeless woman who parked nearby but now possibly, and also impossibly, the daughter of her mother's long-lost best friend.

Gloria was probably not Harriet's daughter, Lexi knew that. It was too much of a coincidence. Her mother knew it too, but if she wanted to welcome Gloria into their family, Lexi would do her best to go along. She pushed away a small tinge of jealousy and wondered instead about how her father would accept Harriet's quasi-daughter in their lives. A daily reminder of his fallibility and shame might even up the balance of power in Number Two Azalea Court. The thought made her smile.

To Lexi's left, Evelyn dozed on the recliner. Gandalf and her wife Jess had fallen asleep on the sofa but left to go to their bedroom an hour earlier. Gandalf—the stiff and aloof woman who never spoke to any of them before the events of this weekend—had looked calm and almost relaxed. Maybe even happy. Even Evelyn looked peaceful, for the moment not telling everyone what they should be doing.

Detective McPhee had left an hour earlier, a little less angry about being suspended from the police department. She had looked like she belonged in the circle. Before she left, before Gandalf and Jess went to bed, the women started planning how they would take over the memorial service in just a few hours, and how that would begin to repair their Azalea Court world.

As she started falling asleep, Lexi realized that the women of Azalea Court probably would never go back to the way it was, each alone around this small circle of homes. They were now connected, woman to woman, bringing the men along even if they were reluctant. Even she, who didn't live on the Court anymore. Even Gloria, who didn't live anywhere. Woman to woman and bungalow to bungalow. She imagined their arms stretched long out of their kitchen windows with their hands grasped across driveways around the Circle. Their circle included the hands of the lost and mostly forgotten women who once lived in this place. Ghosts or not. This weekend, the weekend of her mother running away from her father, of looking for Harriet and finding Gloria, this weekend changed them. The women of Azalea Court had somehow become dear to each other.

SUNDAY MORNING

What We Thought We Knew:
The two day conference ended with artist Anna Schuleit's project to make Northampton State Hospital "sing" by blasting J. S. Bach's "Magnificat" through hundreds of sound speakers at the soon-to-be-demolished Main Building.

—Dr. Sanford Bloomberg,
The History of Northampton State Hospital 1858–1993

Play "Ding Dong the Wicked Witch is dead." Don't play the Magnificat.

—Rebecca Macauley,
former State Hospital patient

THE WOMEN

Sunday, November 10, dawned with the most brilliant sunrise we had ever seen on Azalea Court. Sprawled on beds and sofas in Number Four, we had slept fitfully, exhausted and overstimulated from the weekend's exertions. We woke from time to time, checked on each other, then fell back asleep. Finally, Evelyn roused us all. Jess made coffee and scrambled eggs. Over breakfast we finalized our plans for the Memorial Garden event.

We argued about what to say at the podium. Evelyn wanted Asher Blum publicly accused and humiliated, then arrested for his crimes against Harriet, against Iris, and against herself. She wept as she told us again about the time she was assaulted in the Coach House and how Asher Blum protected the rapist. Gandalf hugged her, awkwardly but with heart, and suggested the two of them think about getting some help dealing with the traumas that haunted them.

At the very least he should lose his license, Evelyn argued, and we all agreed, although it would be largely symbolic at this stage. Not entirely symbolic, Jess argued. He would never be able to prescribe meds to keep a woman quiet again. We sat silently for a few moments, thinking about that.

Then Iris told us that when she returned to Azalea Court after the memorial program, Gloria would come to live with her, at least until she got back on her feet.

Evelyn turned to Gloria, patted her knee, and offered her a job with her home care business. They would get Gloria's nursing license reinstated, and together they'd build up the agency. We all nodded. This was right.

Iris stroked the cat's silky fur. "Canary is coming home with us too."

"But Dad hates cats," Lexi said.

"Yes, he does," Iris said. "But he won't be living with us."

"What do you mean, Mom?" Lexi asked.

"Asher will have to find someplace else to live. Not with me. Not here."

"I don't understand. What will he do?" Lexi asked.

"He'll have to figure that out. How could I live with him, after this?"

We all nodded again. This was right, too. At least some small level of justice might be served.

SUNDAY NOON

What We Thought We Knew:
We thought we knew what mental illness is, but our knowledge was imperfect. We thought we knew how to treat it, but we fell short. We thought we knew how to offer comfort to those who suffer in their brains and hearts. I greatly fear that we were wrong about that too.

—Asher Blum MD,
unpublished manuscript

THE WOMEN

As noon approached, people gathered at the Memorial Garden site. The city had erected a large canvas tent and set up rows of folding chairs, wobbly on the uneven ground. The old stone fountain with carved lions' heads had been repaired and water flowed once again. Many people came from the town, including elected officials and college students, former patients, and former caregivers. Families still mourning their lost members.

Most surprising, every single one of our neighbors from Azalea Court showed up. Donnie and Eric had gone door to door that morning, explaining the importance of the event to our little community and asking people to attend. And they did. Even Aggie and Arnold, who had already started packing their clothing and dishes, their birdhouses and dolls, into cardboard cartons from the supermarket.

Some people came reluctantly. Bea didn't feel much of a connection to the Court or the people who lived there. In fact, she was already thinking seriously of leaving us. Eric had turned out, sad to say, to be a disappointment. She was tired of introducing him as a landscape artist to her colleagues, which didn't happen often, but they couldn't avoid the yearly medical practice party without looking like she was hiding something. She had to accept reality: her husband was just a gardener. Eric sat next to Bea, but he looked everywhere else, as if he also understood their marriage was over. Bea wasn't the woman he thought she was, the woman he needed her to be. He had insisted that Marc and Morgan attend too, but he allowed Marc to bring his tablet as long as he muted the game of slaughter he couldn't stop playing. Morgan was happy to come and moved back three rows to sit next to Aggie, who

251

gave Morgan her favorite doll, Cookie, as a gift, along with a grocery bag of clothes. Morgan couldn't stop smiling.

Aggie divided her attention between Morgan's excited chatter and the new family, Timothy and Winda and baby Imani, sitting in the row ahead of her. Aggie leaned forward on her folding chair, as if she wanted to say something to them, maybe to apologize. But she couldn't summon up the courage or maybe she simply didn't know the right words. Then Imani, held over her father's shoulder, caught Aggie's eye, and grinned. Aggie pulled her hoodie across her face, and then back, playing peek-a-boo with the baby. Maybe she wouldn't insist on moving off Azalea Court right away.

Donnie had helped round up neighbors to attend, but he was terrified of what Evelyn might do or say. Something was changing inside his wife, and he didn't yet know what it would look like, this new willingness to talk about the past. What had shaken loose her frozen self? What would a thawed Evelyn even look like? Watching his wife talking with the new family as if she had known them her whole life, smiling and cooing at the baby, and touching the woman's arm, Donnie almost wished she would go back to the old, mildly bitter Evelyn. At least that way he knew who she was.

Jess and Gandalf hadn't been able to sleep much at all. They had cuddled for hours, whispering, and giggling inappropriately. They looked exhausted but happy now, chatting in the second row with Detective McPhee and her wife.

We filled in the rows of folding chairs facing the portable podium borrowed from the Forbes Library and positioned at the front of the tent. As MC, Jess checked the list of speakers, searching the audience to make sure the necessary people had arrived. Asher sat alone in the front row, all the way on the right, looking through his papers. We all snuck glances at him, wondering what he was thinking, what he would say, how he would react to our plans.

Lexi and Gloria sat at the other end of his row with an empty seat between them. Gloria wore the locket around her neck. Lexi noticed that Gloria kept fingering the small gold heart, and she wondered how her family might change. She wondered how generous she could bring herself to be to this new person in their lives.

Iris waited in the living room of the home next door. She wanted her appearance to be a surprise. To Asher and everyone else.

At twelve sharp, Jess called us to order. One by one, she introduced the speakers, who said the expected things about honoring the lofty aspirations of those who built the state hospital and lamenting how far short of those ideals the reality turned out. The speakers, from mayors to previous superintendents, from former patients to bereft family members, mostly kept to their time limits. It turned out that Rebecca of Rebecca's Way was still very much alive. She told her story and we all wept. We welcomed her into our hearts as a lost woman who was found.

The spoken words wove a tapestry among us all, a canvas of regret and hope, of suffering and resolve. The town committee offered us the opportunity to plant daffodils on the garden terraces after the program. Over time, they promised, the bulbs would spread, to eventually represent each of our fellow human beings who lived and died in the hospital that once stood in our neighborhood and still haunted us.

When it was time for the keynote address by Dr. Blum, we all stole glances at Evelyn, hoping she would swallow her anger as she had promised. She sat next to Donnie, grasping his hand and a balled-up tissue.

Asher shuffled to the podium and began by recounting, with merciful brevity, the list of treatments employed at the hospital over 135 years of treating patients with mental illness: from gyrating chairs to lobotomy, from cold baths to insulin, from cathartics to bloodletting, from basket-making and farming to electroshock therapy and Thorazine and newer drugs. Then he put down his notes.

"Some of you know that I've been writing a book about the treatment of mental illness. I am ninety-four years old and I have been working in this field for my entire adult life. I've come to the sad conclusion that we know—that I know—far too little about why mental illness happens, about how to treat it, often even about how to offer comfort."

"Today is the anniversary of Kristallnacht." His voice grew frail and thin. "The night of broken glass, over a century ago in Germany. That is important to me because it triggered the journey that took me from the Polish shtetl where I was born to a partisan camp in the forest. Eventually, those events brought me here, to America, to my wife Iris. I carried with me one small valise of clothing and a much larger one that was heavy with deep fears. The fears led to mistakes, and then to covering up my mistakes with lies. I did bad things, hoping that those things would protect my family."

We all watched him closely, listened to his sentences swollen with tears.

"The past haunts me. Perhaps it haunts us all," he continued. "Certain events in our history haunt us profoundly, as individuals and as a society. The state hospital that stood right here is part of that history. We are here today to dedicate this garden memorial to help us face our past, in sorrow, shame, gratitude and maybe, someday, joy. Our work as human beings is to do what we can to own our mistakes, to apologize and make reparations, to move forward in life more honestly."

He paused, looking around the audience, then touched his chest with both hands. "I am sorry."

He looked around the audience. "If only my Iris was here. If only I could apologize to her in person."

At that moment, as we had planned, Iris stepped into the tent. It took her a few long seconds to walk with her cane to the podium. Asher looked stunned. She held out her hand to take the microphone from him. She lifted it to her lips and turned to the audience.

"You all heard him, right?"

"I'm very sorry," he said. "Do you forgive me?"

"Not yet. Not even close."

When the buzz of voices quieted, Iris spoke.

"I understand that many of you have been searching for me. Thank you. I apologize for the worry and trouble I caused. Nobody made me leave. Nobody kidnapped me. I ran away to figure out what to do about things that happened in the past, things I just learned about. Those awful things my husband mentioned. I can't make them better, but I can share them with you. Maybe together we can make sure they never happen again."

Iris paused to gather her courage. "So now, I'd like to tell you about my friend, Harriet. She was a chemist and a teacher. She wanted to make the world a better place. We had dreams of raising our children together and working for peace. Who knows what we might have accomplished? Harriet wasn't mentally ill, but she ended up a patient in a mental hospital. Our hospital. She died here, in this place where we now live. She was buried in our field. She was my lifelong best friend and she was one of us. This is her story."

ACKNOWLEDGMENTS

When I moved to the neighborhood built on the grounds of the former Northampton State Hospital, I was already working on this novel, but it was set elsewhere. From my writing desk, I looked across the street at the worn red brick and ancient stone wall of the hospital Coach House. Within a few months, the deep history of this place, and perhaps a few ghosts, convinced me to change the setting of the novel, which in turn transformed the story into something quite different.

Primary source material about the state hospital was critical to my understanding of the history and to imagining this story. I am grateful to the individuals who helped me locate those sources, and to those who shared their knowledge and memories. Thank you, Cheryl Clayton, Judy Snyder, Rebecca McCauley, Julie Schwager, Elise Bernier-Feeley, Elizabeth Sharpe, Laurie Sanders, Marie Panik, Pam Cartier, Robert Fleischner, Michele Reiter, David Lippman, Ellen Nigrosh, Barry Nigrosh, and Victor Caputo.

For readers who want to know more about Northampton State Hospital, I recommend the archives at Historic Northampton and the Forbes Library, and the website www.northamptonstatehospital.org, maintained by Christopher J. Sparks. The hospital's annual reports are available online at https://archives.lib.state.ma.us. Also informative are *The History of Northampton State Hospital 1858–1993*, by Sanford Bloomberg and *The Life and Death of Northampton State Hospital*, with photographs by Stan Sherer and text by J. Michael Moore. To learn about Jewish partisans in the forests of Eastern Europe, I suggest *Uncle Misha's Partisans* and *They Fought Back*, both written by Yuri Suhl.

Archival material can come from unexpected sources. Going through my father's desk after his death, I found a 1948 letter from the Employee Loyalty program of the Department of Commerce, where my father worked as a chemist. The letter requested information about his affiliation with the Washington Book Shop Association. My father's reply indicated that my mother was a member of that organization, which she joined for the discount on purchasing books. Little sparks of history fascinate me!

Once again, I deeply appreciate the experience, wisdom, and energy of publicist Mary Bisbee-Beek and the team at Red Hen Press—Kate Gale, Mark Cull, Tobi Harper, Monica Fernandez, Tansica Sunkamaneevongese, and Rebeccah Sanhueza.

I am very grateful to the members of my long-standing manuscript group, who read multiple drafts of this material and helped me shape it into the novel I wanted it to be. Thank you, Jacqueline Sheehan, Lydia Kann, Maryanne Banks, Kari Ridge, Celia Jeffries, Liz Bedell, and Jennifer Jacobson. Thank you also to my friends Jane Miller, Janet Nelson, and Lesley Peebles, who read drafts and offered their suggestions, and to Amy Romanczuk, whose email in 2002 offered the original spark for this story.

My family has been enormously supportive of my work—listening to ideas, reading drafts, offering feedback, being here. Thank you always, Robby, Jenn, Rachel, Tomas, Josie, Abel, and Carol.

BIOGRAPHICAL NOTE

Ellen Meeropol is the author of the novels *Her Sister's Tattoo, Kinship of Clover, On Hurricane Island,* and *House Arrest,* and the play *Gridlock.* She is guest editor of the anthology *Dreams for a Broken World.* Essay and short story publications include *Ms. Magazine, The Writer's Chronicle, Guernica,* and *The Boston Globe.* Her work has been honored by the Sarton Prize, the Women's National Book Association, the Massachusetts Center for the Book, and PBS NewsHour. A founding member of Straw Dog Writers' Guild, Ellen coordinates their Social Justice Writing project and lives in Northampton, MA.